BOOK 2

LAWMAN

Jim Long: Lawman
By Ronnie Ashmore

Published by Creative Texts Publishers, LLC
PO Box 50
Barto, PA 19504
www.creativetexts.com

ISBN: 978-1-64738-089-2

Jim Long

BOOK 2

LAWMAN

by

RONNIE ASHMORE

For Michele,

for believing when I have doubts.

CONTENTS

PART I

1

Jim Long stepped from the office to the chair that was on the porch. He sat down, tipped the chair back, and propped his boot on the support beam of the awning, taking care not to spill his coffee.

He stared out at the town, his town as far as he was concerned. He was the city marshal. The only law in this town. He looked down at the badge pinned to his shirt. He remembered the man who wore it before, who dishonored what it stood for. Long also remembered how he came to wear it.

He sipped his coffee and looked to his left. His sometimes deputy, Morgan Ritter, came walking toward him. That slow easy gait told Long all was calm in the town.

Morgan was more than a deputy though. He was also a kind of brother. A brother Long never knew of until a few months ago. A brother who at first had tried to kill him.

All that was over now. Their mother, Morgan's father had married Long's mother years ago, ran the family ranch with Morgan helping when not in town.

Long thought back, trying to recall why Morgan would be in town. He could think of no reason.

Morgan stepped onto the porch and looked out at the town, then went inside. A few minutes later he was back with his own chair and a cup of coffee.

Taking a position on the other side of the door he sat down and said,

"How is it so far? Being marshal, I mean?"

Long looked at him with a raised eyebrow.

"You know how it is. Why are you askin' such a thing now?"

"Just thinkin', that's all. Been peaceful around here. That may change."

"Why would it change?"

"Drifter over at the restaurant just now. Talkin' sweet to Frannie. Talkin' loud to everyone else. He looks like trouble to me."

Long looked over to his left, and though he couldn't really, he imagined he could see the restaurant where Frannie worked.

It was no secret Frannie was sweet on Long. Long was sweet on her too if the truth were known.

"That's him over there," Morgan said, motioning with his chin.

The man was dressed in homespun dusty and dirt-streaked clothes that had seen better days.

He wore a pistol in a sash around his waist.

The man made his way into the saloon, shouldering past an old man as he went in. The old man said something, and the stranger gave him a shove. The old man stumbled from the boardwalk and fell to his knees in the street.

Long looked over at Morgan.

"Do you know that man?"

Morgan shook his head.

"Silas shouldn't have the saloon open this early. Folks ain't hardly had breakfast yet," Long said.

"Silas is serving last night's leftovers for breakfast. That's why he's open."

"I'll go see what his story is," Long said, sitting his cup on the railing.

"Want me to come along?" Morgan said.

Long shook his head as he stepped off the porch and crossed the street.

2

As Long approached the saloon, he could hear the man talking to Silas, though he couldn't understand the words.

Long entered the saloon. The man was standing at the bar, a bottle of whiskey in front of him and a shot glass in his hand. The smell of dirty clothes and body odor was hanging in the air.

Silas, the bartender and owner of the saloon stood at the bar, hands on the bartop, looking from Long to the stranger.

The man turned and looked at Long for a moment, then turned back to his drink.

Long took a step farther into the saloon, putting the edge of the bar between him and the stranger.

"What's your name, mister?"

The man looked at Long again. He pushed his hat back on his head and grinned.

"My name is my business."

"You come along and push old men out into the street, it becomes my business."

The stranger noticed the badge for the first time. He sipped his drink, then refilled his glass, raising it in a mock toast toward Long.

"Well, Marshal, I didn't see the old coot. Honest mistake, I swear."

LAWMAN

"Mistake or not. I see you step out of line again; you'll be in our jail. Understood?"

The man gave a mocking salute with his left hand.

"Understood. Jail won't do for me. I have a riding job at a spread north of here. Gotta be there in the morning. So, tonight I'm going to cut loose."

"I said what I wanted. You mind yourself and we won't have any problems."

Long walked out of the saloon. Silas never said a word, just watched the two men talk.

Morgan was still sitting on the porch when Long came back across the street and grabbed his coffee mug.

"I didn't hear no gunfire," Morgan said, following Long into the office.

Morgan closed the door as Long poured himself another cup of coffee.

"A spread north of here. Who would that be? He says he has a riding job waiting for him tomorrow."

"Only one spread would hire a man like that, I'd say. He looks about run down enough to work for 'im too."

Long looked at Morgan, said nothing, just waited.

"The Purple K outfit," Morgan said. "That's the only spread I know that'd hire a fella like him. They are a rough bunch of men out there. Most are probably wanted."

"Who owns the Purple K?"

"Man named Keith. Jacob Keith."

"Never heard of him or the ranch."

"They mostly keep north of here. They don't venture this way much. It would never have been allowed."

There was no response needed for that remark. Both knew too well what it implied.

"We need to keep a watch on this stranger until he's out of town."

Morgan nodded. He couldn't disagree.

3

The stranger sat across the table from three other men. The stranger's cards had been running a little cold, he had been down about fifty dollars. But the whiskey was warm and the ruddy glow on his face along with the deep breaths he exhaled from his mouth, warned the men at the table that he was drunk, and his fuse could be short.

The stranger had started winning. And winning some impossible hands. Hands he should have folded, he came out as having top card. He had made his losses up and then some.

One of the men at the table was an out of towner passing through on the stage. He had decided to sit in on the card game on a whim, to pass time.

But now he was in the hole and couldn't understand why. He rubbed a finger through his thin mustache and called the big man's bet of five dollars.

"Dressmaker," the foul-smelling stranger said. He'd called him that since Isaac had told him his occupation. "You won't believe this, but I got an ace paired."

Isaac stared at the pair of jacks he had been dealt. He couldn't believe the big man was lucky enough to always pair his ace on big pots.

Unless the big man wasn't lucky. Isaac was convinced that had to be the truth.

"What's your name, mister?" Isaac asked.

RONNIE ASHMORE

"Jack. Why?"

"Always pairing that ace aren't you, Jack. Kinda lucky, ain't it?"

Jack sat up a little straighter. He closed one eye so he could focus on the smaller man. The dressmaker was maybe two inches over five feet and was skinny, like he was sick.

"You got something to say, dressmaker, perhaps you should just say it plain," Jack said, not reaching for the money in the middle of the table.

"I've said it. And we have all seen it. You get mighty lucky where aces are concerned. Like it isn't luck so much as it is…"

Jack reached down to the sash he wore around his waist. He came up with a revolver in a flash. He still had one eye closed, only he was using the opened eye to aim at Isaac's head.

"You call me a cheat, you best back it up."

Isaac looked down the barrel of the gun and knew he was in trouble. His heart started beating faster and sweat broke out on his face.

"Now see here, I was just saying, it's uncanny how one man can have an ace every single time…"

Jack shot him. Right between the eyes. Blood and pieces of brain sprayed the two men sitting next to the dressmaker.

LAWMAN

Neither man was a stranger to men getting killed, still they gasped out loud as the pieces of the dressmaker's head hit them in the face.

Jack shoved the pistol back into his sash and looked around the room. Silent stares from the other men in the saloon made Jack laugh. He removed his hat, grinning, as he raked the money on the table into his hat.

"Mighty fine game, gents," he said, standing from the chair and turning for the door.

He stopped in his tracks. He was staring straight down a gun barrel. The grin left his face.

4

Long cocked the pistol as the stranger turned toward him. He saw the look of surprise in the big man's reaction. There was silence in the saloon as men held their breaths watching the lawman and the killer.

"Marshal, ain't no call pointin' that thing at me. I just protected my honor. The dressmaker called me a cheat."

Jack stood his ground. If he were afraid, he didn't let it show. Long wondered if the big man was capable of being afraid.

The only thing keeping Long from breathing heavy was the smell coming from the big man. Stink. Pure body odor.

Long held his pistol steady and stared straight at the man.

"You're under arrest. Walk over to the jail."

"Don't reckon I'm goin' to jail. My new boss won't like that much."

"You're goin'. And if you give me any trouble your new boss can pay for your burial. We clear?"

The big man chuckled, he said,

"You're a tough talkin' ol' boy, ain't ya? All right, I'll walk to jail. You want my gun?"

LAWMAN

Long considered taking the pistol from the sash. In a moment he decided not to in case the man tricked him somehow.

"No, keep it. If you do something stupid, I'd hate to shoot an unarmed man."

Long stood about five foot eight and the stranger was well over six feet. The man looked down on the shorter lawman and shook his head.

Long motioned with his gun and the stranger walked toward the door. They made it to the jail without incident.

Long made the man face away from him and place his pistol on the desk then moved him to the cell. Once locked inside the cage the man sat heavily on the bunk.

"You see to my horse, marshal. He's tied in front of the saloon."

Long sat in the chair at his desk.

"Is that a question or an order?" Long said, looking at the man.

"Take it how you like."

The man pulled off his boots and laid down on the bed. In a moment he was asleep. The room was soon filled with the man's body odor. Long got up and opened the door to the office to let some air in.

It didn't help. It was full dark outside. He could hear the noise from the saloon as if a man hadn't just died over there a few minutes ago. No doubt some men had taken the body of the dead man to the back of the saloon so he could be buried in the morning.

Long saw a couple of horses tied up to the hitching rail in front of the saloon. He looked back inside the office.

The stranger was snoring loudly, the room was filled with a gag inducing odor, and Long could find no reason to stay inside.

He closed the door and stepped off the porch. He would stable the man's horse. He just needed to find which one was his.

5

Long turned the horse over to the hostler at the livery. He left the barn trying to figure out what to do next. He decided it was too late to go calling on Frannie and too early to go to his hotel room.

He went to the saloon instead. He walked in and men nodded at him and spoke to him. Silas filled a glass of beer and sat it in front of him as Long came to the bar.

"Ain't had a killin' in here in a long time," Silas said.

Long looked at him for a moment, then nodded as he sipped his beer.

"I didn't mean nothin' by that, Jim," Silas said.

The implication was that Jim Long's father had been the last man killed in the saloon. Murdered by his brother's father.

"It's fine, Silas. Did you hear a name for the man who did the killin'?"

"Polecat would be my name for him. But the dead man called him Jack."

Long nodded.

"You know the dead man's name?"

"Nah. Skunk just called him 'dressmaker'. He came in on the stage though."

"OK. You ever hear of a spread called the Purple K?"

13

Silas was silent for a moment, then nodded slowly.

"I heard him say that name earlier before you were in. I kept my silence whilst you talked. I heard of it. And Jacob Keith too."

Long looked at Silas and pushed his hat back on his head and smiled.

"You have the same look Morgan had when I asked him."

"Good reason. You may not want to hear this, but Ritter kept trash like that out of this town. Tom would dispatch any troublemaker that came along. Ritter's gone. Tom's dead. Town is still here though."

Long held his first response. He knew Tom was dead because Long had killed him. Ritter was dead because Morgan had killed him.

Instead, Long said,

"You think I can't protect the town?"

Silas didn't answer.

"You asked me to take this job, remember? You and Mayor Tomey."

"Jim, I think you're a good man. A tough man. But I think Jacob Keith has had his way with the north end of this county so long he will figure Leonville is ripe for the taking. Nothing personal."

LAWMAN

Long said nothing this time. He straightened his hat and turned to leave the saloon.

Silas watched him leave. For a moment he felt bad he had insulted the marshal. He liked Jim Long, as did most in town. The demise of Ritter and his foreman Tom had been a blessing to the people. But Jacob Keith could be a plague the town was not ready for.

6

The rider stepped from his saddle and stretched his legs. Even though Buck was the closest thing to a foreman the K had, he had ridden hard to get back to the Purple K Ranch and tell of the news he had heard.

He had been in a little town called Newburg on business for the ranch. The job required him to stay a few days, which he didn't mind. That allowed him to take in the town and see the sights. Although he couldn't remember seeing anything but his hotel and the saloon. Except maybe a saloon girl or two.

The day before was when he heard about

the new man they were supposed to hire. The saloon keeper told the story while Buck was trying to sober up enough to ride.

Hearing that a Purple K man had been arrested sobered Buck up quickly. After an hour of drinking weak coffee the bartender made for him, he had saddled his horse and rode all day to get back to the home ranch.

He saw his boss, Jacob Keith, sitting on the porch. It was near sundown so Keith was sitting on the porch sipping whiskey.

Keith, a man about twenty-five years Buck's senior, was a hard man to work for. Hands came and went regularly. Buck wondered if Keith even knew the hand in question.

LAWMAN

Neither man said anything in greeting. Buck told his story about the new hand as Keith listened.

When Buck was finished, Keith took a long pull from the porcelain whiskey jug he was holding. Tiny rivers of whiskey cut a furrow through the long gray tobacco-stained beard.

"That's what the boys meant by bein' shorthanded. Thought it was because you had taken your lovely time to get back."

"He was arrested two nights ago. Killed some fancy man in the saloon over cards."

"Where?"

"Leonville."

Keith stopped in midair as he started to raise his jug again. He looked at Buck and said,

"Why in the name of the devil would someone go to Leonville and mess up?"

Buck sat down on the top porch step, cursing silently to himself the fact that Keith didn't invite him on the porch or to have a seat in the spare chair.

"Things are different over there it seems," Buck said. "They got a new marshal, and the town seems different from what I gathered from the gossip I picked up."

"Someone should ride over and see if our man is in jail."

"He never worked here, though," Buck said.

Keith looked at Buck for a moment.

"He was hired on and was to report here. He got in trouble while under our brand. He's one of us."

"Well, I'll go tomorrow. I'm beat right now."

Keith stood up, tucking his jug under his arm.

"Today. I want answers by tomorrow. Send the twins."

Keith went inside the ramshackle cabin he called the main house. Buck watched him and then cursed a little louder as he walked to the bunkhouse.

7

Morgan was gone for the evening. He was only a part time deputy anyway, so that left Long having to do the night duty.

Long was tired. The office was just about unusable since the man named Jack had been arrested.

The odors that came from that man were unbearable on their own. But when nature kicked in and he started passing gas it became gag inducing.

So, for the past day Long had avoided the office as much as possible. He'd take the prisoner his meals and empty the johnny pot then retch for a few minutes afterwards to recover. Other than that, he visited a lot of people a lot more often.

He stood on the porch of Frannie's house waiting for her to answer the door. She was one of the people he had visited most often since his prisoner had taken over the jail.

Whether at the restaurant or here at her house, he never missed a chance to see her. Knocking on her door always made him nervous.

She answered the door with a smile on her face, which made Long smile as well. She stepped back so he could enter the house.

She closed the door then threw her arms

around his neck, hugging him tightly. He returned the embrace, happy and content with the way she felt in his arms.

"Long time, no see," she said, stepping back and looking into his eyes smiling.

When she looked at him full on like she was now, Long felt weak and useless. Frannie was quite a woman, and he was lucky to have met her.

Though their meeting could have been under better circumstances, she stood by him through it all and at great risk to herself.

Now, standing in her front entrance in a blue dress that made her reddish hair glow, she looked radiant. Yes, Frannie was quite a woman.

"I just can't go to the office. And I don't want to go to the hotel."

"You really should find a place in town besides the hotel. You are the lawman in town after all, it's not right you being in a hotel."

Long shrugged his shoulders. They had this conversation at least once a week. Long would not change his mind, yet.

"It suits me for now."

She led him to the sofa, where he sat in the middle, she took a position next to him. She was close enough Long could smell her toilet water wafting from her. It was nice, she smelled good.

"Guess what rumor I heard today."

Frannie was always hearing gossip at the restaurant from locals, drifters, and travelers alike. As far as Long knew she never repeated any of it, except to him.

He said nothing. She said,

"We are getting a schoolteacher. Right here in Leonville. A real schoolteacher."

"A what? We don't even have a school."

"Well, Mayor Tomey is going to use the empty building next to the dry goods store as a temporary schoolhouse. Until a real one can be built next year."

"How come I haven't heard of this?" Long asked.

"Are you mad?"

"A bit. The law ought to be kept up to date on what his town is doing. Don't you agree?"

Frannie only shrugged.

"I don't know. But a real school. Can you believe it?"

The town was growing. No doubt about it.

8

Later in the evening Long sat on the porch of the marshal's office and watched the shadows grow along the main street.

Frannie had to go work the supper rush at the restaurant and that had left him with nothing to do. And while he sat on the porch, he had not gone inside the office. He fancied he could smell the prisoner from the porch. Surely he couldn't though.

Two riders approached the office riding different colored horses, but everything else was the same. They wore the same colored pants and blue shirt, the same black hat canted to the left, and sat their horses the same, reins held loose in their left hands.

Long took another look as they approached. They even looked the same. Dark hair in need of a cutting, scruffy beard. Same blue eyes watching Long watch them.

The two men reined up in front of the office porch. Neither man stepped from the saddle. Long kept his seat, watching the men.

"You the law in town?" the one on Long's right asked.

"Marshal Jim Long. Who are you?""I'm Ted, this is Ned. We are with the

Purple K outfit. You have our man in jail. We came to get him," the one on Long's right said.

LAWMAN

"Oh. Well. He can't go," Long said.

"Why not?" the one to Long's left, Ned, said.

"He's in jail. That's why."

"Are you daft, Mister?" Ted said.

Long stood from his chair and looked at both men a moment.

"No, but I think you two are. Now get on out of here before I lose my patience."

"Maybe you didn't hear me. We are with the Purple K." Ted said, slower this time.

Long matched his tone, speaking just as slow.

"I heard you. I don't care. Get back to your ranch. Tell your boss his man is going to stand trial for murder."

Ned started to say something, but Ted interrupted.

"When is the judge due?"

"In two days," Long said.

"Well, we will be back in two days, marshal. See you then."

Ted turned his horse; Ned followed his brother. They rode out of town and never looked back toward Long.

Mayor Tomey came walking up to Long to watch the riders leave.

RONNIE ASHMORE

"Heard that conversation, Jim. It's not good to get the K boys dander up from what I've heard."

"They'll be back in two days, I guess."

"I think you are in some trouble. Trouble this town doesn't need right now."

Long looked at the mayor.

"Afraid your school teacher will change his mind?"

Tomey made a noise in his throat and shook his head.

"Not just the school teacher. There are changes coming to Leonville. Big things are happening. And another fight with a large rancher is the last thing this town needs."

9

The next morning Ted and Ned were sitting around the cook fire in the ranch yard eating breakfast and drinking coffee. They told Buck the story of what happened in town the night before.

Ted took a swallow of coffee and said,

"Young man not much older than me and Ned is the marshal now. Long, Jim Long he said his name was."

A tough looking lean man dressed in dirty homespun clothing looked up at Ted. He said,

"Long you say?"

Ted nodded,

"Yep, Levi. That's what he said his name was. He didn't seem to be impressed with the Purple K brand either."

Buck looked over at the man, he sat sipping coffee, looking into the fire.

"You know him, Levi?"

Levi shrugged.

"Names ain't much out here you know that Buck," he said, staring at the foreman. "Man calls himself whatever he feels like day to day. But I knew a young deputy named Jim Long in Kansas. He worked under Hickok."

"You sound impressed by him." Ned said.

RONNIE ASHMORE

"He was a tough man and good with a gun or Bill wouldn't have kept him on. He was always fair with us drovers who invaded the town every year."

Buck looked at Levi to see if he was going to say anymore. When the man was silent, Buck said,

"No matter. When that judge gets there, we make sure our man is turned loose."

A dozen heads nodded in agreement. Levi watched them all, he figured some even meant it too.

"If this is the same Jim Long, we ain't going to be able to bully him," Levi said.

"You have an idea then?" Buck asked.

"Maybe. First, I need to know if it's him. I'll ride to town and see. Let ya know when I get back."

Buck was silent for a long moment, he sipped coffee and stared out into the morning, looking at nothing.

Finally, he said,

"I like the idea, Levi. Bring us as much information as you can."

"We have until tomorrow before that judge gets there. Can you find anything out that fast?" Ted asked.

Levi ignored the younger man. He stood and went to the barn to saddle his horse. Time like this gave a man time to think, and a thinking man would saddle his horse and ride on out of the country.

26

LAWMAN

But that wasn't Levi Goren's way. Never had been. If the lawman in that town was the same Jim Long that was in Abilene working under Wild Bill, then Levi needed to know.

Levi stepped into the saddle and rode out without a word to anyone.

10

Mayor Tomey came into the restaurant and sat down across the table from Long without waiting for an invitation. Long was becoming annoyed with the mayor, he was having trouble hiding it.

Frannie brought Tomey a cup of coffee, glanced at Long for a moment, smiled then left the men alone.

Tomey sipped the coffee, then said,

"You need to release that man over there in jail."

Long held his fork with steak on it in midair and looked across the table.

"I know you don't want to but there's reasons why," Tomey said.

"What reasons?" Long took a bite and waited.

"The main one is that the man he shot did accuse him of cheating. No one disputes that, not even you. And you can't hang a man for defending his honor."

Long couldn't disagree with what Tomey said so he said nothing.

"Also, tomorrow the new teacher will be here. This is a big step in this town. A teacher all the way from Pennsylvania in little ol' Leonville. We need no distractions of a killing."

LAWMAN

Long considered what was said. It was true nobody disputed the facts of the shooting. It was a justified shooting by current standards.

Nor was the dressmaker the first man to be killed because he overtalked himself and got into trouble.

"I'll consider what you said. It would be nice to air out my office and sit in there again."

Tomey nodded as if the matter were settled. He sipped his coffee then said,

"We are going to have a real school here for the children. You need to consider hiring a full-time deputy to help keep folks from being killed in senseless ways."

Long chuckled, shook his head.

"Can a man be killed in anything other than a senseless way? Where'd you find this teacher anyway?"

"I placed an ad back east a few months ago, after..." his voice trailed off. "Anyways she answered it and I accepted."

"She? You're hiring a woman to come out here and teach?"

"She's qualified."

"You better hope she's homely else you'll see men in this town lining up and fightin' for her."

Tomey looked at him, said nothing, then stood to leave the restaurant. He gave Long a look before walking out the door.

RONNIE ASHMORE

Frannie came out to fill Long's cup again. As she poured, she said,

"What happened to the mayor?"

Long sipped his coffee.

11

After he had finished eating, Long walked over toward the jail. A man was hitching his horse in front of the office, looking around. The right hip of the horse had a K branded on it.

Long continued walking toward the office, he removed the leather thong on his pistol as he went.

The man turned and looked at Long, both men paused a moment in their movements as familiarity sparked a memory.

The man shook his head, then walked toward Long extending his hand.

"Marshal, last I saw you was in Abilene. You had ol' drunk John by the boot heel draggin' him to jail and Wild Bill was laughing at you."

The memory of that moment played in Long's mind. Drunk John was a frequent guest of the Abilene city jail, and he never wanted to go peacefully.

Long smiled, took the offered hand, and said,

"I reckon the whole town had a laugh at that. Drunk or not, John was a scrapper. You'll have to forgive me if I don't recall your name."

Levi shook his head.

"Levi Goren. Abilene was a long time ago, Marshal. I wouldn't remember a drover like me either. I trailed with the Boxed M then."

The name of the ranch meant nothing to Long. Abilene was a long time ago. He had worked there for the last two years of its heyday of being a Cowtown, the last year under Hickok.

Long motioned a thumb toward the horse standing at the rail.

"You riding for the Purple K now?"

"Yeah, winter's comin' on, and I need to not freeze. They are a different sort of outfit, I'll say that."

"I guess I know why you're here then."

They stepped onto the porch of the jail, and Long thought he saw Levi crinkle his nose.

"Boss sent me to see what I could find out about our man being in jail."

Long thought for a moment. He stared out at the people walking along the street taking care of their business.

"Well, it goes against everything I think as a lawman, but I am prepared to turn him loose. He killed a man who apparently sullied his good name."

Levi listened, silently. He didn't really understand what the marshal was saying.

"If I need him, I'll come to the K to get him I guess."

LAWMAN

"Marshal, the Purple K is the last place a lawman should ever want to go. The men he has working there are wanted or will be wanted for somethin' somewhere."

"Why are you there? You wanted somewhere?" Long looked at the man dead on.

Levi was average height, rail thin, and dressed in rough clothes.

"Not me. Thirty a month and found. That's why I'm there."

Long nodded. He saw Levi wrinkle his nose and take another whiff of the air as they moved closer to the door.

"What in tarnation is that awful smell?"

"Your fellow ranch hand. It gets worse," Long said, opening the door to the jail.

12

Levi and his new friend Jack came riding into the Purple K ranch yard as the evening sun was burning hot. Levi rode away from the man as he couldn't stand the smells coming from the new guy.

They reined up at the barn, Levi giving a wide berth to Jack. Buck came from the barn followed by the twins and other men.

Buck started to walk up to the new man, he caught a whiff of the odor coming from him, and halted where he was.

Buck cut a quick glance at Levi who only shrugged and stepped from the saddle.

"Well, I'm glad Levi got you out of jail. Welcome to the Purple K. You work for me and Mr. Keith now. You have no more say in what you do as long as you work here. Clear?"

Jack looked around the ranch yard. The old cabin that needed repairs, the bunkhouse that seemed to lean to the left as if it were going to collapse, and a barn that needed a roof.

"Not much of a spread is it?" Jack said, stepping down from his horse.

"You don't look like much yourself," Buck said.

Ned, standing beside Buck, waved a hand in front of his face. He looked from Levi to the new guy.

"He ain't bunking inside. He could gag a buzzard if he got too close to him.""

Jack looked at the man, started to say something but Buck interrupted.

"No, he won't sleep inside." he looked at the man, "What's your name?"

"Jack."

"Ned, see that Jack is bunked down in the barn."

Buck turned to face Levi, ignoring Jack completely.

"How'd it go in town?"

"No trouble. Long let him loose with no belly achin'.""

"Just like that, huh?"

Levi nodded as he stripped the saddle from his horse.

Buck looked over at the cabin. Keith, leaning against the porch support, was watching them.

Buck walked over to the cabin. Keith watched him come.

"That our jailbird guy?" Keith asked.

"Yes, sir. That marshal just let him loose. Gave Levi no issues."

Keith nodded.

"Makes no sense, does it?"

"What's that?" Buck said, craning his neck up to look at the boss.

"We are going to town tomorrow. You and me. I want to see the changes in this town."

Keith turned and walked into the cabin leaving Buck alone in the yard.

13

Long was sitting at the table in the Rafter R house waiting for his mother to serve breakfast. When he thought about the subject of him being in this house, with a mother he presumed dead, and a not quite brother he never knew, he would get a little flustered. Everything that had happened did so quickly and without much planning on his part.

Martha brought the breakfast platter into the room and set it on the table. She took her customary chair on the long side of the table, across from Long. Morgan sat at the head. This for some reason puzzled Long more than it should have.

"The new teacher arrives in town today, I want to be there to meet the stage," Martha said, putting ham steaks on the plates for the two men.

"Foolish idea to bring a woman out here alone," Morgan said, forking a piece of ham into his mouth.

"Morgan. Hush that talk. She is a qualified teacher from what Mayor Tomey says."

Morgan swallowed his food, then said,

"I know, Ma. But to bring her out here is to ask for a bunch of trouble. Women are scarce here if you haven't noticed."

"Well, at least the town has a lawman that will protect her from these troublemakers. Right, James?"

Long swallowed his food slowly. He didn't want to get into a debate with his mother on this topic, even though he agreed with Morgan's statement. Instead, he said,

"We will do our best," then took another mouthful of food.

Morgan stared at him, Martha stared at Morgan, and Long stared at his plate.

As they hitched the buggy to the horse for Martha to ride into town, Morgan was silent as they worked together. When he had the final harness tightened, he looked over at Long, who seemed to be fiddling with the reins a little too long.

"Could have backed me up in there with ma,' Morgan said.

"She's right, Morg. But so are you. And arguing with each other isn't going to help much in the way of what needs to be done."

Morgan stepped around the horse to Long's side and said,

"What does that mean?"

"We don't know what is going to happen with this whole school idea. Most folks around here seemed to be doing alright teaching their own kids. This idea of needing a school with a teacher in town could backfire on the mayor. In the meantime, the town is growing, with more people expecting more things from it." Long shrugged, figuring he had said too much.

LAWMAN

Morgan kept silent. He looked from Long to the house where Martha was walking toward them. He tapped Long on the shoulder, then nodded toward their mother.

"If it is a matter of support that the idea needs, I reckon Martha Ritter will rally all that is required to make it work."

Long looked back to see Martha, in town clothes, walking toward them, dressed as a Texas version of a queen going to visit the town.

14

Jacob Keith was getting older. He hated to admit it, even to himself. The knees didn't work like they used to, the back hurt more than before, and his nights weren't as wild as they used to be.

He was reminded of all these things as he climbed into the saddle and settled in. He looked over at his foreman, a snarl hiding the grimace of sitting in the saddle.

Buck pretended not to notice. Instead, he said,

"Who all are we taking?"

"Everyone. The town of Leonville will see the Purple K in full force."

Keith reined his horse around and eased over toward the barn. Buck rode up beside him.

Buck gave a nod to the men and in no time all the Purple K riders were in their saddles and ready to go.

Keith led them out with Buck riding beside him, the others followed behind.

After a few miles, Keith looked over his shoulder to his men, then over at Buck.

"What is that smell?"

"I don't know. The wind is behind us."

"Everytime it blows I feel like I'm going to puke last week's supper up. What is that damn smell?"

LAWMAN

"It ain't a what, it's a who," Ned said from directly behind Keith.

Keith reined his horse around and stared at Ned.

"What, boy?"

Ned jerked his head back toward the rest of the men.

"That smell is Jack. We all smell it when the wind catches."

"The new guy? How in tarnation can one man stink so mightily?" Keith spat a wad of chew, then said, "Jack, you ride on ahead of us a few yards. And if the wind shifts you shift with it. Understood."

The men laughed, Buck looked around at them quickly and they quieted. Jack came walking toward the front of the column, his face red from embarrassment.

"No need to call me out like that, Boss," he said as he rode past.

"No need to smell like that, either." Keith said.

Once Jack was a few yards in front the group started off again, this time following Jack.

"We get to town, that man gets a bath. Double soap. I'll pay for it," Keith said.

They rode the rest of the way into town in silence.

15

Jim Long reined his horse to a stop alongside the wagon as Morgan, Martha on the seat beside him, stopped in the middle of the street coming into town.

Long looked around at a town alive with people he hardly ever saw in town before. Women walked along the streets dressed in their Sunday dresses, the men were dressed mostly in their everyday clothes, but there were a lot of people in town.

Morgan whistled as he too looked out onto a busy town.

"There are a lot of folks in town."

Long was annoyed by that useless statement. Anyone could see the town was busier than it should be for a Wednesday. He ignored the remark. Instead, he said,

"I'm going to go see Frannie at the restaurant. I'll see you both later."

Martha motioned with her hand.

"You won't need to go to the restaurant. There she is there. Seems everyone in town is anxious to see the new teacher except for you two boys."

Long said nothing. He spurred his horse to his left and reined up in front of the boardwalk where Frannie stood.

He stepped from the saddle and looked up at her. She smiled a big smile at him as he stepped up on the boardwalk to stand next to her.

LAWMAN

He could smell her toilet water that she wore on special occasions. He thought of mentioning that, then decided that she would chastise him for being a hardheaded man. He didn't need that at the moment.

"Isn't this great?" she said, looking over the town.

"Is it? It seems a lot of people are here to see a woman that may not like the town once she sees it."

Frannie slapped his arm lightly.

"Don't be so negative. All you've done is act like the woman shouldn't be coming here. I think it's a good thing for the town."

Long made a noise deep in his throat but kept his silence.

They moved along the street toward his office. Men greeted him and tipped hats to Frannie. The women seemed to smile a little smile at the two of them as they walked.

Long, not for the first time, felt a little uncomfortable with people in such a crowd. Frannie seemed not to notice.

"I think Mayor Tomey is going to be here when the stage rolls in to meet the lady as well. You should join him."

"I think Tomey can do any welcoming that needs to be done without me."

This time Frannie made a noise in her throat. Long glanced sideways at her. She kept her eyes forward.

Long stopped in his tracks and stared out toward the other side of the street. Frannie walked a few steps before she realized Long was not beside her. She turned and walked back to him.

He looked down at her for a moment, then back out onto the street toward the saloon.

"What's wrong?" she asked, following his stare.

A group of riders were reining up in front of the saloon. They were rough looking, and they were all staring in different directions around the town at the people.

"Those are the last people I expected in town today," he said. "I will catch up with you later. I need to pay attention to this now."

16

Jacob Keith and the rest of the Purple K riders sat their horses looking around in surprise. There were people everywhere.

"All this for a judge coming to town?" Keith asked.

A shout erupted from the crowd as the stage came into view. Folks, men and women, crowded into the street to welcome the noon stage.

Keith glanced at Buck, who only shrugged in response.

The stage rolled to a stop between the general store and the hotel. Only one passenger stepped out from inside the stage.

There was a murmur from the crowd as the young woman stepped down and looked around the small town.

Buck looked at Jacob Keith and whistled lightly.

"Why is she here in this town?"

Ned elbowed his brother Ted, who sat on his horse next to him.

"Brother, I do believe that is an angel, right here amongst us heathens."

Ted said nothing.

The woman was young, in her early

twenties maybe, a small hat was pinned to her dark hair. Her dress, though not new, was nice except for the layer of trail dust on it.

It was her features that sparked all the commotion. She was beautiful.

Levi Goren decided that word was not the right word to describe her. She was more than that.

Levi glanced over at the Marshal's Office and saw Long standing on the porch watching the crowd. He stepped from the saddle and tied his horse to the rail in front of the saloon. He walked over to Long and stepped up on the porch to stand beside the lawman.

"She's causing quite a commotion," Levi said.

Long grunted and shook his head.

"New teacher the mayor hired."

The men watched as her bags were carried to the hotel by some of the men. Mayor Tomey was nodding and smiling while trying to lead the woman from the crowd.

Levi realized too late they were walking toward him and Long. He felt like running but stood his ground instead. He glanced at the men across the street. They were all watching.

Tomey and the woman stepped up on the now crowded porch.

"Marshal Long, I'd like to introduce you to Miss Clara Whitney, the new teacher we talked about."

LAWMAN

Long nodded, and smiled, then said,

"Ma'am, this is Levi Goren."

Levi was caught off guard, but he quickly removed his hat and smiled.

"Miss Whitney, pleased to meet you."

Clara smiled at the two men.

"Same here. It is very nice to know the law is so capable and friendly here in my new home."

Her accent was unlike any the men had heard before. And they liked it instantly.

Before Long could correct her assumption about Levi, Tomey touched her elbow and said,

"We need to go now. Mrs. Ritter is waiting at the hotel for us."

Clara nodded.

"It was nice to meet you gentleman. Marshal," she looked at Levi straight on. "Mr. Goren, I hope to see you around."

Levi had no response. As he watched the new teacher walk away, he was aware of a silly smile on his face.

17

Martha stood as the mayor and teacher entered the lobby of the hotel. Morgan, standing beside her, looked at the teacher, a moment too long. Martha elbowed him lightly, never taking her eyes from the younger lady.

Mayor Tomey, his hat still in his hand, looked at Martha Ritter and nodded.

"Miss Clara Whitney, I'd like you to meet Mrs. Martha Ritter. She is one of your main supporters here in our town as well as the owner of the largest ranch in the county."

Clara Whitney extended a gloved hand which Martha accepted. She nodded, then said,

"Miss Whitney, I hope our mayor has not bored you so far by trying to uptalk our little town here. We have a need for a teacher, and I believe you'll do just fine here."

Tomey's smile remained mostly intact as he realized he had just been rebuked by Martha. If Clara noticed she didn't let on, instead she said,

"Your town is wonderful, Mrs. Ritter. I just met two of the local lawmen outside."

Martha smiled,

"My son, Jim Long, is the Marshal. Though the only deputy I am aware of is my other son, Morgan Ritter," Martha motioned toward Morgan, who only said a quiet hello.

LAWMAN

Tomey, feeling he was about to be upstaged, interrupted further talk.

"Well, ma'am, we need to get you settled in here at the hotel and then I can show you your school, as such."

Martha and Morgan watched as Tomey led Clara Whitney toward the front desk to check in. Martha looked over at Morgan.

"Is there a new deputy?"

Morgan shrugged a shoulder and said,

"Not that I know of. What do you think of Miss. Whitney?"

"I think she is beautiful. I also think she will be a good addition to this town."

Morgan had nothing to say in response, so he kissed his mother on the cheek, and said,

"I need to go talk to Jim. I'll see you later."

18

The men of the Purple K sat in the saloon drinking and talking loudly amongst themselves. Jacob Keith sat in a chair at a table with his foreman Buck, Ned, Ted, and the new man Jack.

Keith looked at Jack then over to Buck.

"I still smell him. I told you I wanted that taken care of."

"Yes, sir, you did. But he don't want to take a bath," Buck said.

"He don't?" Keith said, looking at Jack. "Why not?"

Buck only shrugged as he watched his boss stare at the bigger man, who appeared not to notice them talking about him.

"Jack? That's your name, right? You stink and need a bath, so you're getting a bath," Keith said as he stood up.

Jack looked up at Keith, sneering.

"Boys," Keith said to the rest of his men. "Grab hold of this ripe piece of trash and give him a bath. He fights ya, shoot him."

As one all the men, including Buck, stood from their tables and moved toward Jack. As Jack stood, Buck and a few others grabbed him by the shirt collar and another group pinned Jack's arms to his side.

LAWMAN

The big man was strong, but the Purple K riders were many, and had been given a direct order from their boss.

Tables were scooted roughly from their positions and chairs were turned over, beer spilled as the men grabbed the larger dirty man and began pulling and dragging him from the saloon toward the door.

Jack said nothing, but he resisted being pulled toward the door. There were too many for Jack to fight.

They led him out onto the boardwalk, down into the street where the horses were tied. The horses tried to shy away from the commotion, but they stayed tied to the hitch rails.

The group of men forced Jack to the water trough next to the hitch rail.

Finally, Jack said,

"Ain't no cause you doin' this to me, boys."

"You had your chance. Now we get ours. My orders are to be followed," Keith said, as he nodded to his men.

They all, working in unison, shoved Jack into the water trough, clothes, hat, guns, and all. He made a tremendous splash as he hit the water.

One of the riders had found a cake of soap in his saddlebags, which he tossed into the water with the man.

Jack sat up, spitting and cursing. He looked around at the laughing men standing around the trough. He wanted to kill them all, he wanted to let them know he wanted to kill them all, too.

But before he could say anything, Keith looked down at him, meeting his stare with his own hard look, and said,

"Get to bathin' and don't come out of that water until you're clean. And lose the mean look, you were given an order you defied."

Keith stared across the street to see the marshal was watching them. He turned around and went back into the saloon.

19

Long entered the restaurant just before noon. He felt as if breakfast had been days ago and wanted to eat and relax a little.

Frannie saw him come in, she smiled at him as he made his way to a table. He felt himself blush a little and it annoyed him.

The place was crowded for a noon meal. The noise of various conversations all mingled together to make an indescribable noise.

As he sat down, the Purple K rider Levi Goren came in. Seeing Long, he made his way to the table.

"Mind if I join you, Marshal?"

Long nodded and Levi pulled a chair and sat down.

"What can I do for you, Levi?"

"Been thinking. You saw what the boys did to Jack. What do you think of that, treating a grown man that way?"

Long chuckled.

"I'm hoping that water is still fit for horses to drink after he got done. Why?"

Levi shrugged,

"Seems wrong to me, that's all."

RONNIE ASHMORE

The door opened and Morgan came in, looked around, then walked to the table and sat without invitation. He looked at the stranger, then to Long he said,

"Is this the new deputy?"

Levi stared at the new man like he was daft. Long raised his eyebrows but said nothing.

"The teacher, Ms. Whitney said she met the Marshal and the deputy earlier. It wasn't me she met then, so?"

"Morgan Ritter, Levi Goren. Morgan is my deputy, though I don't know what he's talking about right now."

"Pleasure," Levi said, not offering a handshake. "I ride for the K."

"No kidding? And you're talking to the local law? Jacob Keith may not like that."

Levi stood as Frannie was approaching the table.

"I have to go. We will talk more, Marshal."

Levi nodded to Frannie, then left without looking back.

"What was that about?" Frannie said, watching the man leave.

"Maybe it was something I said," Morgan said, smiling.

"I came to eat. Give me whatever looks good back there and coffee, please."

Frannie looked at Morgan, who shook his head. She nodded, then moved off to the kitchen.

LAWMAN

"You know the Purple K riders aren't here to socialize. You should be worried about what they are doing here."

"Right now, all they are doing is drinking at the saloon, which as far as I know isn't a violation of any known law or ordinance."

Long felt himself growing agitated. He didn't exactly know why. It rankled him that so many townsfolk seemed to be worried about the Purple K riders even being in town. There was nothing he could do if they caused no trouble.

Frannie returned with a plate of food and coffee. As he smelled the food, Long realized he was hungrier than he thought.

20

Levi Goren left the restaurant feeling at odds. He wanted to talk to Marshal Long about his concerns over the Purple K riders and their intentions of being in town. At the same time, he didn't care for that deputy that was always around. Any talking to be done would be done in private, alone.

Levi stepped onto the boardwalk in front of the mercantile, absently walking and thinking. He bumped into another person which interrupted his thoughts.

He was perturbed and was ready to voice his aggravation. Until he saw who he had bumped into.

She stood there in her fancy yet dusty dress, looking at him full on.

Levi grabbed his hat off his head and stood a little straighter as he said,

"Ms. Whitney, my apologies for bumping into you."

"No apologies needed, um… Mr. Goren, isn't it?"

"Yes, ma'am."

"You hardly bumped me at all. No harm done, sir."

Levi felt flustered. A woman talking to him in broad daylight. And not a soiled dove or dance hall woman, but a proper woman. A teacher, nonetheless.

Clara giggled softly at Levi's obvious discomfort.

"I remember you from earlier. With the Marshal."

LAWMAN

Levi only nodded, unable to say anything. This teacher was absolutely stunning. No doubt the prettiest woman he, and many men in these parts, had ever saw.

"Be that as it may, Mr. Goren my question to you is this: When are you going to show me the rest of the town and give me a tour?"

Levi stood there, shocked for a moment. Then said,

"What ma'am?"

"Oh, come now. I believe you hear just

fine."

"Umm…Well…I ain't a deputy," he said, feeling foolish for having blurted that out for no reason.

Clara stared at him for a moment, then laughed quietly into her gloved hand.

"Is that the answer to my question or one that you were asked earlier this evening?"

"I mean, I heard you thought I was a deputy. I ain't."

"The proper phrase is 'I am not', we can work on your grammar later. After you take me around town for a tour."

She walked off leaving Levi standing on the boardwalk, hat in hand, looking and feeling like a fool.

Why would she want to go around town with a man of his ilk? He was nothing but a saddle tramp, a gambler, and a lover of the low kind of life.

RONNIE ASHMORE

He put his hat on, then made his way to the saloon. He needed a drink, never mind the fact that the Purple K riders were still in the saloon carrying on.

It embarrassed him to realize that he was officially one of those riders.

21

Jacob Keith sat watching the man called Jack. Jack had come in from his impromptu bath in the horse trough and taken a seat at the far end of the saloon. He sat there alone and drinking the rest of the time.

Jacob got up and walked over to the table Jack occupied by himself. He sat down across from the man without an invite.

"What are you thinkin'?"

"It wasn't right to embarrass me in front of the men like that."

"You stunk. What else was to be done?"

"I have to kill 'em now."

"Kill? Who?"

"All of you. Not now, but when the time is right, you all will die."

Keith stared at the man a moment, then stood and placed money on the table.

"Anytime you want to try, son, feel free. In the meantime, here's the wages you're owed. Don't come back to the ranch."

Keith went back to his original seat next to Buck and sat down. He leaned in close to Buck and said,

"I just fired Skunk. You and the boys better watch him though, he ain't right."

Buck glanced over to where Jack was sitting drinking his whiskey in silence. He met Buck's stare.

The front doors swung open, and Levi came in. When Ned saw Levi, he sneered at the man and made a noise in his throat.

"Look! Levi took time from making friends with that law dog to come drink with us," Ned said.

Levi ignored the comment. The Ned said,

"I saw him talking all sweet to that lady, the new teacher. Why would she want to talk to a no account like you, Levi when other fine men like us are available?"

All the men laughed at that remark. Levi looked at Ned.

"You keep talking like that and someone will shut your mouth for you, Ned."

Ned stood, his hand near his pistol butt, a smile on his face.

"It won't be you, saddle bum. You wanna try?"

"Sit down!" Keith yelled.

Ned looked at Keith. Buck had both hands under the table. Was he holding a gun there? Ned stared at Levi as he sat back down.

LAWMAN

"Levi, you have been too friendly with that lawman. I don't want a man on my payroll that has any connection to the law."

Keith took some money from his shirt pocket and gave it to Buck, who handed it to Levi.

"Your wages. Now, be gone so we can get drunk in peace," Buck said.

Levi took the money, not bothering to count it. He silently turned and walked out of the saloon.

22

Clara Whitney stood looking out over the town from the porch of the hotel. She still could not understand why she chose to give up everything she had back east to come to a small dirty town in Texas. It seemed irrational that she would actually do it.

The advertisement in the paper for a town in search of a teacher seemed so exciting from her comfortable room she had been living in. Now?

It would be difficult to adjust to her new surroundings. Dirty men dressed in rough clothes that hadn't been laundered in weeks, women in plain clothes that had no fashion sense compared to the women she had known.

That wasn't entirely true though. The older lady, Mrs. Ritter, seemed to be a woman who knew what she was about. And wealthy too, if the mayor was to be believed.

The mayor, Tomey, now, was a study. He greeted her in a suit Clara was sure was his nicest, but it had seen better days. The cuffs were starting to fray, the sleeves were worn at the elbows.

She sighed deeply, then smiled. This is what she had signed on for so she shouldn't be complaining about people who would be her new friends.

She turned her head to the left and saw that cowboy, Levi Goren, coming from the saloon. There was something about him. The way he acted, nervous just being around her, hardly able to form a sentence. It made her laugh inside. He was so different from the men she had known previously in her life.

She saw him look in her direction and stop walking. He tipped his hat, grinning. He came walking toward her, slowly and almost hesitantly.

As he approached, he took his hat off and stopped at the bottom of the porch, looking up at her. He looked nervous.

"Ma'am, begging your pardon. My afternoon just freed up some, if you'd like to walk around town with a saddle bum, I'd be mighty proud."

Clara hesitated a moment, looking him over. He was the exact image of what she had just been thinking so critically about. A rough man in rough clothes.

"Mr. Goren, you come walking up and just ask me out of the blue to go strolling around town with you, a complete stranger. What kind of woman do you take me for?"

"Ma'am?" he said, his nervousness on full display as he turned his hat in hands.

She stepped forward, and said,

"I'm teasing you. I'd be delighted to be shown the town, Mr. Goren."

He smiled as she stepped off the porch, her dress held in her hands. They walked side by side as Clara waited for him to say something. He seemed to not know what to say, so Clara said,

"Mr. Goren, this will be a long walk if we do not converse."

Levi looked over at her for a moment, the unasked question plain on his face.

"Talk, Mr. Goren. If we do not talk."

"Ma'am, I ain't sure what to talk to a lady about. I wouldn't want to make you mad if I said something wrong."

Clara looked up at Levi and smiled. He was different from any other man she had known back east. Most of the men she had ever known were confident, sure of themselves. Something about this man's uncertainty was very calming.

23

Jim Long got up from his desk chair and walked to the window and looked out toward the saloon. Nothing different from the last few times he had looked.

He could hear the raucous laughter and tangled voices when he opened the door to step out onto the porch.

The Purple K riders had been in the saloon drinking all afternoon. Long expected trouble from the men but so far there had been none.

He saw the new teacher and Levi Goren walking around looking in store windows and seemingly having a nice chat. That seemed odd to Long. He reminded himself to mention it to Frannie later.

At the saloon the batwing doors swung open, and men began coming out on the steps. Men began stepping into the saddle of their horses.

Long watched as they mounted, glad they were leaving town.

One of the men, the young one who was the twin of the other, stared at him from across the street. Long didn't know his name, Ned or Ted. he couldn't tell.

"You starin' at me, lawman?" the man said, walking out into the dirty street.

Long was silent, watchful.

RONNIE ASHMORE

"I ain't scared of you marshal. You should know that. Purple K riders ain't scared of nobody."

A big man stepped forward along with the man's look alike. They grabbed the drunk man, as the twin said something.

The big man spun him toward his horse and pointed. Then he looked back at Long.

"Boy can't hold his liquor. He meant no harm…yet," he said.

Long remained silent. Jacob Keith reined his horse around to stop in front of Long. He looked the town over.

"We will be back, and we expect more hospitality than what we feel this town has shown us."

"I don't know anyone who wasn't hospitable to you," Long said.

From behind Keith, in the tangle of riders, the drunk man pointed over toward mercantile.

"Look. It's that pretty teacher," he said.

"Ned, shut up and ride out, now," Keith said, still staring down at Long.

The riders headed north out of town. As Keith started to rein away Long said,

"Keith. You're welcome here until you and your men cause trouble."

Keith laughed a bit, then squinted down at the marshal.

LAWMAN

"We go where we want. Remember that Marshal."

Keith spurred his horse to catch up to his men. He didn't look back.

PART II

24

Long sat at the table with Frannie in her house. He had watched as she had set the table and now, she sat down to eat the meal she had prepared for them.

"This sure smells good, Frannie."

The house was hot and stuffy from the heat of the day and the fire from the meal preparation.

"Thanks. I have been wanting to do this for you for a while. It seems you're always busy."

Long felt a pang of guilt at her choice of words. He knew he could have, should have made time for her. But he still wasn't sure how he truly felt for her. Or her for him, though he had an idea.

"It should be better now for a bit."

It was all he could think to say. Frannie smiled at him; he felt his heart race. She had that effect on him, and it aggravated him more than he could say.

"Is everything settling down?"

Long nodded as he shoved a forkful of food into his mouth. He swallowed, then said,

"Seems so. Ms. Whitney is getting her room ready for the children. They are working on it every day."

"I see your friend, Mr. Goren over there a lot, helping out."

"Goren ain't my friend. I hardly know him. He seems like a decent fella though."

Frannie swallowed her mouthful of food, then said,

"Mayor Tomey seems to be taking an interest in Ms. Whitney. From what I see she is only paying attention to Mr. Goren though."

Long gave a short chuckle.

"Makes no sense to me. Why would she be interested in Goren."

"Who knows why a woman takes to a man. Besides he is kind to her from what I've seen of them together. And she seems to enjoy his company."

"He's a saddle bum."

"Maybe it isn't about what he has," Frannie's voice rising as she stood from the chair. "Maybe it's about what she feels when he's with her. And maybe she just wants to be romanced in any form that may take."

Frannie tossed her napkin on the table and walked from the room. Long sat chewing his food watching her walk away.

He thought she would come back in but after a few minutes he knew he was alone. Strange, he thought. Why would she get mad at what he had said? He thought of the conversation they had had but couldn't find any reason for her being mad.

He got up, his food half eaten, and left the house quietly.

LAWMAN

25

Jacob Keith led his men down the street to the saloon. Buck riding next to him kept his eyes roving over the town, looking for any changes since the last time they were here.

Buck saw the marshal step from his office onto the boardwalk and watch the men ride up to the hitching rail in front of the saloon. Buck ignored the lawman's stare.

Keith dismounted and looked his men over then nodded at Buck.

"All right, boys. Let's drink this place dry and have fun," Buck said.

The men gave a shout and dismounted. They headed into the saloon in a hurry.

Keith stopped as he entered the saloon. At a far table was Jack, the man he had fired after they had forced him to take a bath in the trough in front of the saloon.

Jack looked up from his beer glass and glared at Keith and then Buck.

"Bartender, whiskey all around. Except him," Keith said, still looking at Jack.

Silas, the bartender, began pouring shot glasses of whiskey.

Keith downed his in one motion, placed the glass on the bar hard, then looked at Jack.

LAWMAN

"You still mad? Surprised to still see you in town."

"I'm here. Told you I would kill you for what you did," Jack said, slurring his words.

Silas refilled Keith's glass and said,

"Don't mind him, he's been drinking most of the day."

Keith looked at Silas.

"Shut up." He looked over at Jack and said, "Well, here we are. Ripe for the killin'."

Jack stood up, balancing himself by placing his hand on the table. He touched the butt of the gun in his waistband.

"Ned." Buck said, conversationally.

Ned stepped up to stand beside Keith. He held his whiskey glass in his left hand. He unhooked the leather thong from his gun with his right.

Jack stared at Ned, then said,

"I kill him, you all will kill me I guess."

Keith smiled.

"Boys, if stinky here gets past Ned, we will turn around and ride out of town. Peaceful like. Understood."

Jack grabbed for his gun. He was smiling as he reached for it. The smile faded as he pulled it from his waistband.

Ned already had his out, and firing. Ned's first bullet hit Jack in the chest causing him to drop his gun, unfired, to the floor. Ned's second bullet hit Jack in the throat.

RONNIE ASHMORE

Jack fell across the table he had been sitting at, knocking it over and spilling the beer on the floor.

Ned holstered his gun as Long came in, gun in hand.

"All right, what is happening?"

"Happened, Marshal, not happening." Keith said, turning back to the bar. "Stinky drew on Ned."

Long looked at Silas, who nodded.

"Jack drew first. It was stuck in his craw the way they treated him last time."

Long holstered his gun. He looked at the twins. He couldn't tell one from the other.

"I'll send someone for the body," Long said, as he turned and walked out of the saloon.

26

Levi Goren was busy painting the final area of the wall of what would be the schoolhouse. He disliked this kind of work, feeling more at home on horseback, but Mayor Tomey was paying thirty dollars for the renovation of the building.

Levi had worked for a week getting the building ready. After this coat of paint, it would be ready. And he would be glad to be done with it.

A light knock on the open door made him turn in that direction. A smile came to his face as he turned to see Clara Whitney standing in the doorway looking at the work that had been done.

She looked at Goren, a smile on her face as well.

"You have done an excellent job, Mr. Goren."

He took his hat off and nodded.

"Thank you, ma'am. It should be ready for you come Monday."

"I was curious if you have eaten today. I made a simple picnic lunch for us to enjoy, if you're so inclined."

Levi stood there silently for a moment caught off guard. He smiled at Clara, then said,

"I'd enjoy that, sure enough, ma'am."

RONNIE ASHMORE

They stepped outside, Clara in front, Levi following. On the boardwalk they met Jim Long walking their way. Clara smiled as the marshal approached.

"Hello, Marshal. How are you today?" she said.

"I came to see how Levi was coming along on the room, ma'am. I guess you're off to somewhere else now, it seems."

Levi was in no mood for small talk. He was anxious to get on with the picnic Clara had mentioned. He didn't want her to change her mind or Long to know he was going on such a thing.

"We are having a picnic," she said.

Long stood there silent, hoping the surprise didn't show on his face. He looked at Levi, who seemed to be trying to hide in his own skin.

Levi caught Long's look. Changing the subject, he said,

"I heard shootin' a bit ago."

Long nodded.

"One of those twins from the Purple K shot that fella Jack. Seems to be self-defense from what Silas says."

Levi looked at Long then at Clara.

"Ma'am, excuse us for a moment, please."

He walked away from where Clara stood, Long followed. He kept his voice low to make sure Clara didn't hear him.

LAWMAN

"Marshal, those men mean nothing but trouble to this town and you."

"Oh, how do you figure that?"

"I heard talk when I was out there. Jacob Keith is a mean man if I ever saw one. Those twins, Ned and Ted, are like the enforcers for the bunch."

Long nodded. He glanced over at Clara standing alone on the boardwalk.

"Well, for now they were in the right it seems. Go enjoy your picnic with Miss Whitney."

Levi walked over to Clara. They left the lawman standing alone. Levi looked back over his shoulder once.

Long was crossing the street back to his office. From the boardwalk in front of the saloon, one of the twins stood in front of the saloon watching him and Clara. Because of the distance it was hard to tell which one.

27

Ned stood watching the saddle bum, what was his name again? It didn't matter. The man didn't interest Ned at all.

That pretty woman walking with the man did. She was by far the prettiest thing he had seen in his whole life.

He looked over his shoulder. The others were still inside the saloon drinking and telling lies to each other seemingly unaware of the beauty that was amongst them at the moment.

He saw the man look back after speaking with that marshal. Ned decided to follow to see what they were going to do.

The woman stopped at the restaurant and picked up a basket of something. They headed toward the livery.

Ned went to his horse in front of the saloon. He tightened the cinch, then appeared to be fussing over the buckles and reins, all along he was watching the woman and man.

As the hostler hitched a buggy for them, Ned stepped into the saddle. As the buggy rolled out of town, Ned followed behind, slowly. A plan formed in his mind as he rode.

He didn't stay too close to the buggy. There was no need for that, following the trial would be easy enough if he kept his distance.

LAWMAN

They made their way to a spot that overlooked the river but was covered in shade from the cottonwood trees.

Ned reined up under a huge cottonwood and watched the two climb from the buggy, the man helping the lady down.

A picnic. What a nice spot for one if you were into such stuff. Ned never could understand such things. He had never had a woman that he didn't rent by the hour and until he saw the lady he was just fine with that situation. Now though, he was thinking differently.

He wished he had brought whiskey with him from the saloon. There would be no time to get some later.

He dismounted and tied his horse to a limb. Slipping his pistol from his holster, he catfooted his way toward the two, who now sat with their backs to him on a blanket facing the water.

He slowly walked close enough to hear their conversation, which seemed pointless to Ned.

Ned stepped on fallen small branches which snapped loud enough to cause the man to look around.

Ned raised his pistol at the man, whose name he remembered now. He looked from Levi to the lady then back as they both stood.

"Hate to interrupt such a good time but the lady is coming with me."

"That's not going to happen, Ned or Ted, whichever you are," Levi said, stepping forward.

RONNIE ASHMORE

Ned pulled the hammer back on his pistol causing Levi to stop.

"You're not armed. You came out here alone with her without a way to protect her. That's fine with me. Makes it easier for me."

Ned shot Levi twice. One bullet hit him in the shoulder, the other hit him in the side. Levi fell to the ground as the woman screamed.

Ned smiled at the lady as he walked closer to her.

"You are a coward, sir. Shooting a man without means of protection."

"You sure talk funny, lady."

Ned hit her in the face, closed fist. She crumpled to the ground.

28

Jim Long adjusted his seat in the chair. He sat on the porch of the office watching the town but mainly keeping an eye on the saloon.

The Purple K riders were still in there, drinking and making a ruckus. Though so far it had all been good natured fun. Nothing like the warning Levi Goren had given him earlier in the day.

The riders came out of the saloon, all in a group. They each mounted their horses still talking amongst themselves.

Jacob Keith and his foreman came out last looking the men over. Keith placed a hand on a support post for balance and with his other counted his men.

He looked over at Long, then said something to his foreman standing beside him, who nodded and mounted his horse as well.

The foreman said something to the others, and all turned their mounts and rode out of town on a run. A cloud of dust rose in their wake and slowly drifted off in the hot evening.

Keith stepped up on the porch, his eyes locked on Long. Long stood to avoid being looked down upon as they spoke. Keith nodded toward the jail door.

"All right, let's have him."

"Who?"

"My man. He wasn't with us just now. He went out earlier and never came back."

"I don't know who you're talking about."

"Marshal, I will make life hard on you if you mess with me and…"

Long took a step forward, getting within inches of the older man.

"Keith, I don't have your man or anyone else in my jail. But if you don't ride out of here now, I'll make room in there for you."

Keith didn't back up. Instead, he said,

"You think you're a tough man, Marshal. Well, I've seen tougher."

"Either way, I don't have your man in jail."

Keith paused for a moment, nodded, smiled, then turned and stepped off the porch. He went to his horse, adjusted the cinch, then mounted. He rode out of town fast, not looking over at Long again.

As Long sat in his chair again, a wagon came rolling in fast kicking up dust. The driver was slapping reins to the two horses even as they entered town, he was yelling at the top of his lungs for the marshal. He came to a sudden halt in front of the office, the trial of dust following. Long turned his head a moment as the dust passed.

"Marshal, man's bad shot here," the man said, jumping from the seat to the ground.

LAWMAN

Long met the man at the rear of the wagon.

Levi was lying in the wagon, unconscious, blood covered his shirt.

Long gave a bystander an order to go get the doctor.

"Where'd you find him?" Long said.

"Liked to not. He was off the path in a clearing by the river. Passed out like this," he pointed to the man.

Long looked at another bystander.

"Go get Morgan. Tell him to go get the sheriff from Center and bring him here." He looked around, pointing to three men. "Take him to the doctor, now."

Long watched as they carried Levi away. The wagon driver looked at Long.

"Lucky I found him. Didn't see no sign of the woman though."

Long looked at the man not understanding.

"Looked like a picnic to me, Marshal."

Then Long remembered.

29

Long looked the area over. The man who had found Levi Goren had led him back to where he'd found him. Under normal circumstances it would have been a nice place for a picnic. But now.

Now the blanket was strewn about, covered in blood which was drying fast in the heat. The basket that contained the food had been foraged by animals, pieces of chicken and other things scattered about.

There were buggy tracks, but the buggy was gone. Long followed the tracks, the tracks went north, then he saw it.

A horse had been tied to the buggy. The tracks of both were clearly visible. The boot print of the man who tied the horse was clear as well.

Long measured the size against his own. The heel of the man's boot was worn down on the outside. Long made a mental note of that as he rubbed out his own print.

He looked the area over again then mounted and headed back to town.

When he got back to town, he discovered the gossip wheels had been turning. The hostler, an old man named Julius, met him at the stall Long was placing his horse in.

"That teacher is missin' and Goren is still not awake."

LAWMAN

That information figured to be floating around town. Clara Whitney would be the only one who could get Levi to go on a picnic. And the gossips in town would know that.

Mayor Tomey met Long as he came out of the barn. Tomey looked pained.

"This is bad, Jim. Real bad," Tomey said as he fell in stride beside Long.

"I know. I will find her, Mayor."

"Do you know who did this? Who shot that man and took Clara?"

Long knew or at least suspected. He also knew to keep his suspicions to himself until he met with the sheriff.

"I'm on my way to talk to Levi now," Long said as he quickened his pace and left Tomey standing in the street.

Talking to Levi wasn't possible as he remained unconscious the rest of the evening. Long stayed at his desk in case there was a change in his condition.

At around midnight, Morgan walked into the office. Long stood from his desk as Morgan closed the door.

"Is the sheriff outside?"

"He's probably in bed at this hour, I don't know."

"What?"

Morgan sat heavily into a chair across the desk from Long who remained standing.

"He ain't comin'."

Long sat down, staring at Morgan.

"That makes no sense. The shooting happened in the county. That's his job."

"Told him that. He said the people involved are townsfolk. And townsfolk are your business."

"But I think I know who did it."

Morgan waived a dismissive hand.

"Then we will have to deal with it. He's not much use anyway. He was blind drunk when I got there. Passed out in his own jail."

Long could think of nothing else to say. The whole incident took place out of his jurisdiction, so technically he had no right to investigate it.

Flustered and at a loss, Long sat silent. He felt the weight of the town's expectations fall heavily onto him.

PART III

30

Ned sat in a straight back chair in the small cabin and stared at Clara Whitney, a smile on his face. She had come around slowly after he had knocked her out. The bruise on her face was an ugly blue. But it would heal soon enough, and that face would be as flawless and angelic as before.

She struggled with the rope that held her hands behind her back. Her feet were tied together, and the extra length of rope was tied off on the wood stove.

"Quit strugglin'. You ain't goin' anywhere."

He stepped over to her and kneeled. As he removed the gag from her mouth he said,

"I take this off you're gonna want to scream. But don't do it. No one can hear you where we are anyway."

Clara didn't scream. She looked Ned in the eyes the whole time. As the gag was removed, she said simply,

"You needn't have hit me."

"'Needn't'? What kind of talkin' is that?"

"Educated."

Ned laughed.

"You're a spitball aren't ya? We are gonna get along just fine."

"If you're going to kill me, I'd rather you do it now."

LAWMAN

Ned stood up, forcing Clara to look up at him.

"I ain't killin' ya. No, I aim to marry ya. After you lose some of that wildcat in ya."

Clara stared dumbfounded at him.

"What makes you think I'd marry you? I saw you kill a man that I was fond of."

"Well, the way I figure you're free to marry now since he's dead."

Clara sat silent fighting back tears. She was scared. But if he really wasn't going to kill her, she might be able to find a way to escape. She had to keep her wits about her.

"You will never get away with this. There are laws even in Texas."

"Law don't matter much out here. I'm a Purple K man. We sort of make our own laws."

"Where are we?"

He smiled at her.

"A long ways from anywhere. Even if you got loose, you'd not know which way to go for help. Like as not, you'd be lost and die out in those woods."

Clara slumped a little as the man talked.

"Who are you?" she said.

RONNIE ASHMORE

"Names don't matter much here in these parts, ma'am. What I'm called here won't be the name you take on our wedding day."

Ned walked to the lone window and looked out. He turned toward Clara, kneeled again and tightened the ropes that held her.

She resisted when he tried to place the gag in her mouth again. He raised his hand, threatening to hit her. She allowed herself to be gagged.

"Sun will be up in a hour or so. I need to be gone for the day. I'll be back this evening sometime to check on you."

Ned leaned in and kissed her softly on the brusied cheek. Clara made a noise from behind the gag.

Ned stood and went to the door. He turned to Clara as he put his hat on.

"Don't go anywhere now."

When the door closed as he went outside, Clara silently began crying.

31

Jim Long and Morgan were on the trail as the sun came up. Long had filled Morgan in on what he'd found at the site and what Jacob Keith had said prior to Levi being brought to town.

"So, you think you can just ride into the Purple K and Keith will fall down in a fit of confession and turn over his man?"

"He can save his confession. He has a man he couldn't find at the same time the events happened. It's worth a conversation."

As they topped a rise overlooking the Purple K ranch they reined up and looked over the scene below.

Long saw men already working though the morning was still new and fresh. Hands were walking to and from the barn. Horses were being gathered and saddled. At the ramshackle house Long saw Jacob Keith sitting on the porch.

Long spurred his horse down the hill, Morgan following. As they rode into the yard, men stopped working to watch the pair.

Jacob Keith stood, waiting for the lawmen to ride up.

"Marshal, any business we had was taken care of in town. 'Preciate you leaving my range," Keith said as he stepped off the porch.

RONNIE ASHMORE

Several men gathered around and watched. Long only recognized the foreman, Buck and one of the twins. Long ignored Keith and instead addressed the twin.

"Which one are you, Ned or Ted?" he said to the man.

"I don't likely remember, Marshal. Sometimes I can't tell us apart," the man said, taking a step forward.

Some of the men laughed.

"I'm looking for your brother. Keith said he was missing yesterday."

Keith stepped up to Long's horse and placed a hand on its neck.

"You wanna talk to my men, you go through me or my foreman. Don't address them directly."

Movement from the barn caught Long's attention. He looked at Morgan and nodded over that way.

The missing twin came walking toward the cluster of men. It irked Long that he couldn't tell one from the other. The man walked up and stood beside his brother.

"Did I hear this local law dog say I was missing?"

The mood of the men changed instantly. Long could feel it in the air. It would only take the word from Keith to start a shooting match between the hands and the lawmen. Long looked down at Keith and said,

"You found him I see."

LAWMAN

"He was bored with your town and rode out to Center to have some fun," Keith said. "Now, suppose you tell me what this is about."

Long considered it for a moment.

"Local woman is missing, and a man was shot down. We are looking for her."

"Here? On my ranch? Marshal, I have tolerated you long enough. We don't have a missing woman and we didn't kill anyone in your town."

Long made no attempt to correct Keith. He looked at the men in the group. All he saw was hostility and an eagerness to fight.

"I told ya once to leave. If I have to tell ya again the boys will make you leave. Understood?"

Long sat for a moment, then turned his horse around and rode out of the ranch yard. Morgan followed.

32

Clara Whitney sat on the floor tied up and gagged, tears running silently down her cheeks. She questioned why she ever left the comforts of her nice home back east to come to this wild, forsaken place. She thought herself a fool.

The man had said he wouldn't kill her. But she would rather be dead than think of anything else he had planned for her.

Her mind went to Levi Goren. To see him shot down like that, no warning, no reason. It was frightening. To think of him being dead hurt her more than she could ever express.

She looked around the room. It was sparse. A bed against one wall. The mattress was stuffed with some sort of grass to give it some comfort. A small table the man had sat at earlier. A wood stove sat against the far wall. It was this she was tied up to, which ensured she couldn't get loose.

She tried moving her fingers, but her hands were tied behind her back and bound tight enough she couldn't move them. Trying caused her pain.

She had no concept of time. A curtain blocked the one window so she couldn't see out. Even if she could see the shadows, she would not be able to tell the time. All she knew was she needed to go to the privy.

She tried to think of other things other than the growing pain in her lower belly. She thought of her rescue.

LAWMAN

Rescue? No one knew she was here, wherever here was. With Levi shot down and dead in the area they were going to picnic, and her not being well known in town yet, she had no hope of rescue.

The dark-haired man who took her could do what he wanted, and nobody could stop him. He had said he wanted to marry her. That thought sickened her. She needed to keep calm and figure a way out of this.

Then what? The man was right. Even if she got loose, she had no way of knowing where to go for help.

As her thoughts kept hammering her, she fought back the tears. She needed to be strong.

The pain in her belly grew stronger. She couldn't cross her legs to help fight the urge. Not that it would help anyway.

She glanced around the room again. It was as sparse and ugly as her situation. She couldn't fight the tears any longer. She felt them coming.

She stopped fighting and let go of what dignity she had left. As the tears started to fall, she lowered her head, relaxed her lower belly.

Crying hard through the gag, she voided her bladder on the floor where she sat. The release of both fluids did little to make her feel a little better.

33

Jim Long sat at his desk, Morgan leaned against the wall by the window. They were both thinking of what had happened at the Purple K earlier that morning.

"Maybe you're wrong," Morgan said.

Long looked up at him, considered the statement, then shrugged.

"Maybe. What else makes sense though?"

The door opened in a rush as Mayor Tomey came into the room in a fluster. He looked at both men then threw his hands up and pointed at Long.

"What are you doing in here? There is a woman missing. An important woman in this town, by the way."

"We are working on it, Mayor."

"Jim, look, I know you're a young man. We know why you have this job. But this is the kind of thing that ruins people's reputations. Do you understand?"

"I'm not worried about my reputation, Mayor. Are you worried about yours?"

Morgan giggled under his breath, a look from Tomey silenced him.

"Find Miss Whitney. Now," he said, turning and walking out of the room as fast as he walked in.

LAWMAN

Morgan whistled lightly as Tomey closed the door. A short moment later a young boy came into the office. He looked from Morgan to Long, then said,

"Marshal Long, the man is awake. I was s'pose to tell ya that. I don't know his name though."

Before the boy finished speaking Long and Morgan were out the door heading to the doctor's office.

Levi was laying with his eyes closed, his head on a pillow that was flattened by the weight.

He opened his eyes and looked over as Long and Morgan entered the small room that served as the doctor's recovery room.

"Dr. Neils says you're lucky to be alive," Long said as a greeting.

"Ms. Whitney? What happened to her?" "She's missing. We don't know."

Levi looked over at Morgan, then back at Long.

"One of the twins. I don't know which one."

Morgan stepped closer to the bed.

"We went out to the Purple K. Both were there."

Levi shook his head.

"I'll be ready to ride in a little bit. We can go back."

34

Ted sat on a rise overlooking the cattle that were feeding in the small valley below. From a distance he saw Ned riding toward him in a slow easy gait.

Ned had always been a concern. First for their parents, then for Ted. Ted considered himself to be the level-headed one, the one who considered the consequences of whatever he was about to do. Ted had killed men for money and for sport, but he always needed a reason.

Ned on the other hand was reckless, impulsive, and mean. He enjoyed killing, enjoyed hurting people. As a result, they both had enjoyed a home at the Purple K. It was their home.

Ned rode up and sat next to his brother and began watching the cattle as well.

"What did you do?" Ted asked.

"All I been doin' is some thinkin'. I'm thinkin' I'm not long for this place anymore."

"What does that mean? This is home."

"Was home. Now I figure I need to go off someplace else and start over."

"You took that woman, didn't you?" Ted asked, his voice soft.

Ned ignored the question. Instead, he said,

LAWMAN

"A man ought to be able to go off and find happiness anywhere he chooses."

"You did take her. You damn fool. Mr. Keith will not stand for harmin' a woman. Not even from you."

Ned looked at his brother for the first time since riding up. He pointed his finger and said,

"Ain't nobody harmed nobody. I shot that fella dead because he had what I wanted. Now, Mr. Keith ain't never had a problem with killin' a man."

"OK. We have to protect each other. Like always. That marshal was out here today, maybe we threw him off by both of us being here. We have to stick together."

Ted took his hat off and scratched his head, then said,

"I don't want to know where she is or

what you're doin'. But whatever you do you better do it fast."

Ned looked at his brother and smiled.

"That is my whole plan. But you can't tell anyone. If the boys know I have that woman, they will all want a chance with her."

"I ain't tellin' nobody. But brother, you better be prepared to kill a lot of men for a long time if you do this."

35

Jacob Keith sat at his desk. He ran his hands over it as he thought. He had made the desk himself; he had wanted a large desk because that was how he saw himself; a big man should have a big desk.

He leaned his elbows on the desk, it wobbled under his weight because of the legs being uneven. He stared across at the desk at Buck.

"I don't like that town dog comin' out here. He thinks he can just ride in here and talk down to us."

Buck stayed silent. He knew his boss was upset; he also knew that when Jacob Keith got upset people got hurt.

"You gonna say anything?"

Buck adjusted his seat in the chair, then said,

"Just thinking, that's all. He says a woman is missin' and a man dead. Also, you said Ned was not with us when we rode out of town."

"So?"

"Maybe the lawman is right. Ned took the girl, shot the man, and brought that kind of trouble here."

Keith leaned back in his chair and waved a dismissive hand.

"I couldn't care less who the men get into a scuffle with. Hell, all the boys have killed men."

LAWMAN

"Yeah, I know. But you know the woman makes it different. You hurt a woman nobody will have sympathy for you."

"Have you got a plan or you just belly achin' like a woman?"

"If Ned did something to that woman, then Ted knows. We get the truth from both of them."

Keith stood up and ran a hand over his bearded face. Buck stood with him.

"It's been a while since we had us a good war, huh Buck?"

"You think that's what this is building to?"

"We will make sure of it. Talk to the twins. That law dog will be back unless I miss my guess. When he does come, we welcome him with both barrels."

"Ain't killed a lawman in a long while, boss. You sure?"

"Marshal Long invaded our home. We must defend it if he comes back."

"And the woman?"

"If Ned has her. He shrugged his shoulders, "We don't know that he does. One problem at a time."

36

Long stood in front of his office. He didn't really know what he needed to do. He thought about the morning. He knew what happened to Levi and Clara Whitney, he just couldn't prove it. Not for the first time, he cursed the sheriff for not coming to handle this situation. Morgan came from inside the office and stood beside his brother.

"What's the plan?"

Long shrugged.

"I don't have a plan. We go riding back to the K those men will be wanting a fight."

"They need one if they know Ms. Whitney is kidnapped."

"Just you and me? Not much of an army against those men out there."

"I'm sure we can rally the town folk if need be."

"This isn't their fight. They pay us to enforce the law what kind of message would that send if we started asking for help when trouble came?"

"Then what do you want to do?"

"I'm going to the Purple K and snoop around."

"Alone? You just said they'd want a fight, now you're going off alone out there?"

"If I do this right, they won't know I'm out there."

LAWMAN

Morgan threw his hands up in the air and turned his back to Long. Turning to face him again, he said,

"You're loco, you know that?"

Long did not argue that point. It was crazy to even think of riding near the Purple K range and snooping around.

Morgan walked away without another word. Long turned to go the other direction and saw Frannie walking toward him.

They had not spoken since she got upset during the meal a few nights previous. Long tried to read her emotions as she walked up. He was unable to.

"Any word on Ms. Whitney?" she asked.

"None. Any rumors in town of note?"

Frannie shook her head.

"Jim, I'm worried about the woman. If she did fall into the hands of the men from that ranch like they say, then she is as good as dead."

"Folks think the Purple K men got her?" Frannie shrugged.

"They know you two went off out there this morning early."

"I'm trying to form a plan right now, Frannie."

"Only one plan as far as I'm concerned. Go get her and bring her back."

RONNIE ASHMORE

Frannie turned and walked away leaving Long standing on the porch.

37

Ned stepped through the door of the small cabin. The smell of urine mixed with something stronger hung in the air almost choking him. He left the door open to air out the room. "You OK? Did you pee yourself," he said, as he knelt in front of her.

He removed the gag, saw the streaks on her cheeks where her tears had dried. She must have cried a lot since morning.

He waved a hand in front of his face.

"Smells like you messed yourself as well."

Clara watched him silently, not wanting to answer the man at all. He grabbed her chin with his finger and thumb and raised her head as far back as he could.

"That's OK. We got a crick you can wash yourself off in."

Ned stood and looked down on the woman. He kicked her leg lightly with the toe of his boot.

"Woman, you need to talk to me when I say something. A wife should be able to talk to her husband I figure."

He untied the rope from the stove, then untied her hands. Clara made no effort to resist, she knew it was useless to fight the man.

He tied the long rope around her waist and held the end in his left hand.

"Let's go get cleaned up. You smell almost as bad as skunk did before I kil't him," he said, nudging her out the door.

It took her eyes a moment to adjust to the sunlight. She squinted and put a hand up to shield her eyes. The movement hurt her arms; her hands were tingling as blood returned to her fingers.

As they walked a few yards to the creek, Clara looked around at the woods and rolling terrain that she was surrounded by.

At the water's edge she looked back at her captor.

"You're going to watch me?" she said, hugging herself with both arms.

He laughed and pushed the hat back on his head.

"I'm not letting you outta my sight. Your clothes need a washin' too, so just get on it there and wash."

She untied her shoes and removed them slowly. She looked back at the man, then stepped into the water fully clothed.

"I'm hungry," she said, as she waded further into the creek.

Ned gave the rope a hard jerk. Clara fell into the water with a splash. She got up wiping water from her eyes and face as Ned laughed.

"I got you some food, don't worry."

LAWMAN

Ned was laughing and having a good time at her expense. Clara fought back the tears in her eyes as she tried to wash the stains caused by her bodily fluids from her skin.

38

Later that evening Long had a plan in mind. He had saddled his horse and headed back to the range of the Purple K. He had no intention of riding into the yard as he had done earlier.

This would be a fact-finding trip which hopefully led to the location of Clara Whitney. Mayor Tomey had stopped him on his way out of town and made some empty threats and pledges as to what the town expected for their money.

Long ignored the politician. This was about more than money or what a certain person thought.

Now, hidden in the trees on a rise above the ranch, his horse picketed a few yards behind him, Long watched the ranch yard.

From this distance it was hard to see details of who was who, but he dared not get any closer for fear of being seen.

The men all seemed to be doing their evening chores and getting ready for the night. There was little doubt the Purple K had a nasty reputation as an outlaw operation but Long wondered what the reputation was built upon. Killing and robbing for sure, he had heard those rumors in town from some of the old timers. Rustling? Most likely.

No telling how many cows Jacob Keith had on his range and how many dozens of calves each produced in a year.

Long smiled at his own joke as he wiped sweat from his brow.

LAWMAN

As the sun started to set and shadows grew long, he went to his horse and got his bedroll. He spread it out under the trees. He would need to be up before the men down there were moving around.

Early the next morning he was up before sunrise. He was irked that he had no coffee to start his day. He sat up and looked down at the ranch.

The activity was just getting started as the men began moving around. He watched as they made breakfast and had coffee. His mood didn't improve watching them have what he didn't.

He started to roll up his bedroll when movement to his left caught his eye. Far off a lone rider came toward the ranch. Riding easy, not like a man who'd rode night herd.

Long watched as the rider dismounted and accepted a cup of coffee from another man.

Long wished he could tell who it was, but the distance was too far. What did it mean?

Nothing? Something? No way of knowing. No there was a way of knowing. It involved being sneakier and more careful than Long might be capable of.

And he would need help.

39

Clara sat tied to the stove once again, her hands behind her back. The man had left early this morning. It seemed he was in a foul mood.

Clara didn't know why.

After her impromptu bath last night, he had let her air dry in the warm evening breeze, slight though it was. Now, her clothes smelled, she could smell her own body odors, and she knew she would have to mess herself again. Which might make the man even madder than he was now.

Clara had always, from an early age, felt that she was beautiful. Always the prettiest girl in whatever endeavor she chose to do. From primary school to college, she was always so sure of her beauty.

Now, she was beginning to feel that beauty was vain and useless in a place like this. If she were unable to escape from the man, then she would find another way out.

Her mind fluttered with thoughts of Levi Goren. How different he had been compared to other men she had known in her life. He was kind, respectful, and always a little nervous around her. It was the calm feeling he made her feel whenever they were together.

The picnic had been her idea, to try and get him to open up and talk about serious things with her. It was a good idea at the time. Until that man had shown up and killed him.

LAWMAN

Clara looked around the room again. How could she get loose. She had never been the strongest girl, but that was during games of fun, like Tug O' War and such as a child.

Now it was a matter of living or dying. And she did not want to die in the middle of nowhere Texas alone and smelling like urine and feces.

She pulled her legs up. The rope around her feet pulled taught against the stove. She pulled harder, pushing her weight on her back against the wall. The rope held fast.

The stove wobbled though. A little. Maybe enough, if she kept working with it. She pulled harder, straining under the pressure of the rope around her feet.

Sweat broke out on her face, she could feel her face turning red with the effort. She strained harder for a moment. She relaxed, taking a minute or two to catch her breath.

She pulled again, harder. This time the stove leg wobbled and moved a little bit.

Encouraged by this mild achievement, she rested. As she sat catching her breath, tears rolled from her eyes. She pulled hard one more time.

The leg of the stove gave way. The leg was pulled toward her and hit her thigh. The stove fell over, pulling the smoke flue with it to the floor in a crash. Ashes scattered everywhere and created a mess.

Clara sat there for a moment, stunned. She had had the strength to break free from the ropes that held her. She worked her hands down her legs and got them in front of her. She untied the knot.

She stood, looked around the room, then headed for the door. Without a glance back, she went outside. Free.

40

Long looked at Morgan, then back at Levi Goren, who was walking, albeit slowly, across the street toward them.

Long and Morgan stood in front of the livery saddling their horses, Morgan had seen Levi coming and said as much to Long. When Levi was within ten yards, Long said,

"You should be in bed."

"Maybe. But I'm goin' with you," he said stopping to catch his breath.

"I told you we could handle this," Long said, stepping closer to Levi.

"Marshal, this ain't about whether you can or can't. It's about Clara. What happened to her was on my watch so to speak. I'm goin'," he said, motioning for the livery man to bring him a horse.

Morgan shook his head.

"What's between you and her anyway?" he asked.

Levi looked at him for a moment, then pointed a finger at him.

"Morgan, I respect your brother as I knew him in the wild days. I don't know you. Don't ever ask me a question like that again."

Morgan considered a reply. A look from Long stifled it. The livery man brought Levi his horse. Levi climbed in the saddle slowly and wincing in pain, though he tried to hide it.

Once he was seated in the saddle, he looked at Long.

"So, you're going. Are you going unarmed?" Long asked, stepping up in his own saddle.

"I was hoping you'd loan me the use of a gun or two. And maybe deputize me."

Morgan just looked at Levi who returned the look.

"I ain't never killed a man in anger. If I kill that twin out there, I want it to be legal."

"We ain't goin' to kill anyone, Levi. We are going to go find Ms. Whitney and bring whoever took her to justice."

"There's all kinds of justice, Jim," Levi said, spurring his horse toward the marshal's office.

Long and Morgan followed behind. Morgan went inside and got a pistol, a rifle, and more ammo. He handed these to Levi.

"If this country is to have any chance for growth where respectable folk like Ms. Whitney would want to live here, there has to be laws. Real laws, not something made up at the end of a gun because someone's mad," Long said.

Levi snapped the loading gate closed on the pistol Morgan had given him then placed it in his waistband. He looked at Long, then said,

LAWMAN

"Spoken like a true lawman. I'm ready." The three rode out of town without another word, Long leading the way.

41

Clara stood in front of the small cabin and looked around at nothing but trees and rolling prairie. She knew from her excursion last night where the river was, but she hesitated to go in that direction.

Though her experience was less than none in wild country, she figured it only mad sense that her captor would look for her around the creek.

She looked around. Behind the cabin was a slight hill with trees and woods covering most of the ground. She decided it was in that she would go.

Gathering her skirts in her hands she ran; she stumbled once then continued. At the base of the rise, before climbing up it, she looked back toward the cabin.

She was shocked to see her shoe tracks on the ground, as clear as the sky. She panicked, then composed herself.

She decided to go back in her own tracks to the cabin. Walking backwards, she made it to the cabin. It was a slow process.

She then went to the creek and backtracked the same way. It was tedious and wasted a lot of time. The man usually came back around dark, she had no idea when that would be.

Choosing each step carefully so as not to leave a trail, she walked to the rise again. This time when she looked back, she was happy to see even she didn't know which track to follow.

It wasn't much, it would set the man back a few minutes, meanwhile she had wasted precious time. She had to find civilization; people who would help her get back to Leonville.

She went into the woods climbing to the top of the rise. She stopped to catch her breath. Disappointment set in as she realized there was another, bigger rise in front of her. Determined she pushed on.

More trees, more plants that stuck her legs, scratching and drawing blood. Limbs with huge thorns ripped at her once pretty dress, tearing gashes in the fabric no tailor could ever fix.

It was dark and shadows were long in the cover of the trees as she climbed higher. There was a smell to the earth that reminded her of her mother's root cellar back home. Thinking of home threatened to bring tears.

She shook her head and climbed on. She made it out of the trees and vegetation to the top of the rise. As she came clear of the trees, she was greeted with a view that took her breath away.

She stood looking over the country. It seemed to her she could see the entire state from this point. Movement caught her eye. She squinted against the setting sun.

A lone rider. Heading in the direction of the cabin.

42

Ned stood looking over the wreckage in the cabin. The stove was lying on the floor, the flue lay on top pointing at him like an accusatory finger.

Ned swore loudly, then kicked the stove. The metal was unforgiving and prompted another round of swearing as he walked off the pain in his foot.

He stepped out into the yard; he searched the ground for any sign. He saw tracks heading to the creek. He began following them. He heard a horse approaching. He turned to see his brother riding up.

Ned was already angry now he grew belligerent as his twin rode up to him.

"What do you want, Ted?" Ned stood with his hands on his hips, staring.

"Wanted to see this girl you plan on marryin'." Ted stepped from the saddle.

"She's gone ain't she?"

"How would you know that?" Ned asked, stepping closer to Ted.

"See tracks going to that rise yonder," Ted pointed at the ground then the rise.

Ned stepped over to the tracks, he kicked dirt over one and cussed again.

LAWMAN

"Tracks goin' to the creek too." He laughed a small laugh, "Knew my gal was a smart one."

"Smart enough to get you in trouble. We need to find her. We also have to tell Mr. Keith."

"No, I don't want to tell him, Ted. He will be mad for sure."

"You wanna see mad, don't tell 'im and let a passle of lawmen, maybe even Rangers, come riding into his yard and him caught unawares," Ted said.

Ned considered what Ted said for a long moment. Then said,

"OK. We tell him. Then we come back out here and find her. She's on foot and don't know which way is which."

"The boys can help."

Ned stepped up into his saddle and stared at his brother.

"Ned, once we tell Mr. Keith it becomes a Purple K matter. You know when that happens, she won't ever live to see a wedding day. Not with you or anyone else."

"Maybe I can change Mr. Keith's mind," Ned said, spurring his horse back toward the ranch he had just come from.

"And maybe you can teach that horse to fly," Ted said as he caught up with his brother.

43

Jacob Keith listened to Ned tell his story. Ted and Buck stood against the far wall silently watching the old man.

Keith never interrupted Ned, he allowed him to tell it in his own time and way. When Ned finished speaking Keith looked over at Ted.

"You know about this?"

"Found out today, sir."

Keith stood and looked at Ned, who had trouble holding the old man's intense stare.

"That lawman will be back. Might bring his friends along. You and your stupid actions have put this place in danger. Now, you fix it." "I didn't mean for her to get away. Hell, she can't go far."

Keith walked to the window and stared out at the men working at the barn. Without turning around, he said,

"Buck, Ted. Go tell the boys to saddle up and take whatever ammunition and guns they have. We will send someone back for supplies as need be."

When Ted and Buck left the room, Keith turned to look at Ned.

"I cared for you, son, like you were my son. I don't condone what you did. But you will fix this."

"Whatever you need me to do, sir."

LAWMAN

"When we find this woman, you will be the one to put a bullet in her brain. After you and the rest of the boys have their fun."

Ned stood silent, shock on his face. Keith laughed.

"It ain't so easy to make up for this kind of wrong."

"You want me to kill her. I want to marry her."

Keith laughed a short laugh.

"Won't ever be a marriage, son. You hurt a woman out here you might as well forget about a future if anyone finds out. So, the only way to ensure no one finds out is to make everyone a party to it."

The words finally hit home to Ned. He nodded his head a bit, then shrugged one shoulder.

"That makes sense. We find her, we have our fun, I'll kill her."

Keith waved a dismissive hand signaling the meeting was over. As Ned left and the door closed, Keith ran a hand over his bearded face.

He felt like a man on borrowed time. Try as he might, he couldn't shake the feeling.

44

Long and his party rode up on the same hill overlooking the ranch Long had used previously. Though unlike then, there was no movement at all from the ranch. Nobody came from the barn; no sounds of men or animals could be heard.

Morgan looked at Long then at Levi.

"He don't look good."

That was true enough. Levi looked to be in a lot of pain. He was sweating, and breathing hard, every jostle of the horse caused him to moan slightly.

He had not complained once since starting the trip. He just kept going.

"He's fine," Long said, not looking at Levi. "What is bothering me is that down there."

"They're gone," Levi said, his voice gravelly and low. "Maybe on a raid or rustlin' party."

Long looked back at Levi.

"No, I never went with them on those," Levi's answer to the unasked question.

"If they ain't there, we should go have a look-see," Morgan said.

"Let's just sit and wait a bit," Long said. "I'm tired of sitting and waiting. The woman is here somewhere and they ain't. Let's do this," Morgan said staring at Long.

"I agree with Morgan. I ain't got much sittin' in me. Let's go down there and see what we see."

"You two are in a hurry to get shot at."

Long spurred his horse down the rise. Morgan and Levi followed behind. In the ranch yard, Levi stayed in the saddle as Morgan and Long searched the buildings.

Long went to the house and opened the front door, expecting to get shot at any moment. As he entered the old house, he yelled Clara's name.

Only silence greeted him. The house was eerily silent, which unnerved Long a little.

"No one's in the barn either," Morgan said behind him.

Long jumped a little. He hoped it didn't show, then said,

"House is empty too."

"Saw a mess of tracks going back northward though," Morgan said, motioning that direction.

Outside, Long looked in the direction Morgan pointed. The same direction the lone rider had come from earlier as Long watched from the rise.

"Anything of note that way, Levi?"

It took about ten seconds for Levi to respond.

"An old-line shack that's only used in the winter months."

"If I was gonna..." Morgan started to say.

Long interrupted.

"Let's go."

45

Clara had no idea what to do or where to go. She had watched the first rider then the other ride into where the cabin would be if she could see it from where she was. Then she had seen them ride off together the way they had come.

She could only guess what that meant. And she was out of guesses. That seemed like hours ago. Now she was hungry, and as the sun began sinking lower and lower, she was becoming frightened.

She didn't know what kinds of wild animals lived in the woods, either back home or here in Texas. She had never been a nature or woods loving girl.

She made a silent vow that she would learn to love the woods if she were to survive this.

She looked around at the woods. Tall trees, that is what she saw, and the brush with those blasted thorns that had cut her clothes and flesh as she climbed up the rise.

She lightly rubbed a hand over a few of the scratches as she looked around. She wandered toward a tall tree. Then sat down. She didn't know what she should do. If she were to survive it would be up to her. There was no help coming.

She chided herself for being such a wilted flower. Back home she was known as a tough lady, one who brooked no argument, or accepted no insult.

RONNIE ASHMORE

That was back there in another land. Where tough was measured by a different ruler than out here. Here toughness was based on actions not words or attitudes.

She got up and looked around once more. Sitting here and being an easy target wasn't the answer.

She looked in the direction the riders had ridden off in. If they went that way, then trouble lay in that direction.

She started down a small trail that only small animals could use. She followed it anyway, mainly because it went in a direction different from the one the enemy had taken.

The path led back down the rise. For a moment fear gripped her insides. Replaced a moment later by a sense of dread.

She was heading down the backside of a hill she had worked so hard to climb up. For what?

Nobody knew where she was or if she was even still alive. People in town may have thought she went back east, that the small town wasn't meant for her.

All these thoughts flooded her mind as she continued to put one foot in front of the other and make her way slowly through the brush down the hill.

46

Jacob Keith rode at the head of the group of men, Buck beside him. Keith motioned to Buck, and they fell to the rear of the group, the others going ahead.

"What's wrong?" Buck said.

"Nothing yet. I want Ned to kill that woman. I want you to see he does it."

"OK. Any reason to think he won't."

Keith shook his head.

"Him and that brother of his has been with me a long time. They have done things the right way. Until recently."

"This woman, you mean?"

"It started a while back. Ned is too quick to want to kill, lately. That cowboy we ran into on our last roundup? It caused us a delay in our work."

Buck nodded, remembering.

Roundup was Jacob Keith talk of rustling. The roundup involved other men's livestock. None in this county, all in other counties. Roundups happened two or three times a year.

They would take the young stuff, change a brand, if need be, then let them grow to size on the Purple K range.

The older stock would be driven to market in the spring or sold to ranchers in this county.

RONNIE ASHMORE

While folks whispered and talked as if they knew where the cattle came from, no one ever openly accused Jacob Keith and the men of the Purple K of rustling. At least not more than once.

Ned and Ted served as the enforcers on the range. They took care of any problems that arose and threatened the ranch. From simple threats, to beatings, even killing. It was their main job on the ranch. And it was work they took pleasure in.

"Taking this woman though, that was too far. We might stretch a rope if caught with the cattle operation, but to harm a woman will kill whatever we have built here," Keith said, breaking into Buck's thoughts.

"You have an idea, I assume?"

"Yeah. Kill Ned when this is over."

"You want me to kill Ned? What about Ted?"

"I haven't thought that far yet."

Buck reined up causing Keith to stop as well. Buck dismounted and walked a few yards from Keith.

"What's wrong?" Keith said, from the saddle.

"Killin' Ned won't be an easy task. He's mighty slick with that gun. And I don't know that he fears anything."

Buck looked up at Keith.

LAWMAN

"Killin' Ned won't be an easy task. He's mighty slick with that gun. And I don't know that he fears anything. And then there's Ted."

Keith stared out ahead, silent. Then pointed back the way they had come. Three riders, still just dots on the landscape, were riding in their direction.

Fishing in his saddlebags, Keith pulled a pair of field glasses out and looked. He recognized two of the riders. He lowered the glasses, looked at Buck, then said,

"Gather the men. We got company comin'."

47

Long lead the way across the valley. On each side hills rose but the trail they followed kept straight ahead. He pointed to a large hill covered in trees and brush.

"Looks like a good place for an ambush. Keep a look out," he said.

Morgan glanced at Levi. He seemed to be barely sitting on his horse, weaving like he would fall off any second.

"He still looks bad. I think he's bleeding," Morgan said, causing Long to look back at Levi.

Blood was leaking through the bandage on Levi's shoulder, seeping through his shirt. Without a word, Long turned left, leading the group into the trees at the base of a low rise.

Long dismounted and touched Levi's shoulder, causing the wounded man to wince in pain.

"Damn, Jim. I'm OK. Let's keep goin'."

"You need to rest here. Me and Morgan will take it from here. Where is the cabin from here."

Levi tried to laugh. It sounded like a pain filled snort instead.

"You won't find it. Besides, they're up there somewhere. Probably close to findin' Clara as we lollygag here."

LAWMAN

"Levi, in your condition you'll slow us down," Morgan said.

"We ain't been making record time til now anyhow."

"OK," Long said, mounting up. "Let's go."

The party was once again on the move through the valley. Morgan kept looking over at Levi to check on him. After several looks, Levi said,

"Morgan, I will make it to see this through, count on that young 'un."

Up ahead on a hill something flickered. Was it a rifle barrel reflecting the sun? Long grew uneasy, as if he could feel the rifle pointing at him, waiting to fire the kill shot. He cursed the open terrain they were riding through.

"Pay attention. I think we've been spotted."

The other two sat up straighter, which was hard for Levi, looking in all directions for danger.

"That cabin is on the other side of that rise yonder," Levi said, pointing in the direction they were headed.

"Any shortcuts?" Morgan asked.

"That is the shortcut."

Long pulled his rifle from his saddle scabbard, Morgan did the same, Levi didn't even try.

"All right, they probably have ten or twelve men up there with them. Us three are no match for that. We can't engage the whole bunch. We need Ned. He's the one we're after."

"Brother, I don't reckon they'll just let us ride up there and get ol' Ned so easy like."

Long didn't answer. The three kept going.

48

Jacob Keith stared down the large rise and watched the men come on. The sun would be down in a couple of hours. Darkness would help his men a lot.

He walked back to where the rest of the men were seated or standing by their horses. Some eating jerked beef, some just sitting in silence.

All of the men were tough in their own way, they would steal what they wanted before they would work for it, but few were killers. This was a time for killers.

Keith wondered how many would stand strong through what needed to be done.

"They're a comin'. We need to get a welcome prepared for them," Keith said, kneeling in the dirt. His knees protested the effort, a groan came unencumbered.

Picking up a stick, he drew circles in the dirt. Eventually, he looked up at eleven faces staring back at him, waiting.

"OK. Here's what we are going to do. Findin' the woman is more important than that lawman behind us. So, get to the cabin, pick up that trail, and find her."

"We ain't sure where she went," Ned said.

"I know. When you get to the cabin, split up." He motioned to a couple of the men standing around, "You take four or so men and follow the creek trail. Buck, you and Ned follow the other trail."

RONNIE ASHMORE

Keith stood signaling there would be no discussing what the orders were. Keith caught Buck's strange look and nodded at him.

"That marshal is out here chasing us. Who's minding the stores back in town? That's what I want to know?"

Buck shook his head in disbelief.

"You thinkin' of robbin' that town now? Of all times, now?"

"I don't know when there'd be a better time."

"How about not now. We have a problem on our hands at the moment," Buck said.

"She's a Yankee woman lost in the woods. We can find her easy. That town is ripe for pickin' and I aim to pick it."

Buck turned away from his boss, the look of disgust clear on his face.

"Buck, we find the girl, we get this lawman, then that town is ripe for us to clean out."

"What do you want us to do?"

"Ned stays here with me. You take Ted and the other two and find that woman. Bring her to me."

Ted smiled, then looked over at his brother. Ned was not smiling. He was watching Buck and Keith wondering what was wrong between the two men.

Buck glanced over at Ted, shook his head. He turned his horse and said,

LAWMAN

"All right, men. Let's go."

49

Clara Whitney stood at the bottom of the rise she had just walked down. As she caught her breath she looked around at the valley.

The shadows were growing longer down in the valley than higher up on the rise. It would be dark soon, and she was growing concerned.

She had no way of knowing what to do. The man was right. Escaping was a foolish idea. She was lost in these woods and would die here.

She decided to walk, direction or reason didn't matter now. Just to move. To feel as if she were in control was all that mattered.

She heard a horse nicker. Was it? She looked around, saw nothing. As she topped a rise, she jumped back in fear. A horse and rider were there. The rider sat watching her, a smile on his face.

It was the man who had taken her. He smiled at her, then shook his head.

"Buck," he shouted over his shoulder. "This gal is so lost she'd prob'ly walked into our camp if we'd waited."

His voice was different yet the same. That was what Clara noticed before she fully comprehended his words. Something was different with his voice.

LAWMAN

Another rider came up. Both men dismounted, watching her.

"This was easy enough. We might get back to camp before dark."

The dark haired one pulled his pistol and cocked it.

"We kill her or what?"

"Put that away, you damn fool. The boss wants to see her."

The man holstered the pistol. So, the man called Buck was in charge. He acted like he was in charge. The way he carried himself as if he were sure of what he was saying and doing.

The dark-haired man followed orders as he was given them.

The two men stepped closer to her, then winced at the smells coming from her. Clara noticed. For a moment she was embarrassed.

"We got to get her back to camp," Buck said.

"How? She has no horse."

Buck grinned.

"She can ride double with you."

They stepped toward her. Clara considered resisting, or running, or something. But it all seemed futile. She had tried that and yet here she was a prisoner again.

In the end she offered no resistance as they tied her hands in front of her and placed her on the other man's saddle.

As he climbed up behind her, he made a gagging sound.

"Whew, by God, she smells rank."

The one called Buck looked back and laughed at them.

"Not as shiny as she was in town, is she?"

He spurred his horse and led them off. In the same direction she had been walking. Clara silently cried.

50

Long looked back at Levi Goren. He looked worse than he did earlier. Morgan ignored Long's glance at him.

"All right," he said, stopping his horse near a grove of trees.

The other two stopped as well. Long dismounted and with Morgan's help got Levi out of the saddle and laid on the ground.

"What are we doing?" Levi asked, his face showed the pain he was in.

"We are going to go find Clara. You are going to rest here until we get back," Long said.

"You ain't leaving me here. I won't allow it."

Long looked down at him.

"If you can get on your horse, you can follow us," Long said, nodding toward Morgan who was tying Levi's horse to a tree limb twenty yards away from where he lay.

"Damn, you both."

Morgan placed a canteen next to Levi, then said,

"We will be back as soon as we can."

They remounted and rode off without looking back. Both men were scanning the countryside for enemies.

RONNIE ASHMORE

After riding about two miles, Long was getting nervous, Morgan could sense it.

"What's wrong?"

"Night is not our friend, Morg. We are on their land, they know where they are, we have no idea where we are."

A rifle exploded and Long's horse went down hard, throwing Long from the saddle. He hit the ground and felt the air rush from his lungs. He managed to kick his left boot free of the saddle as his horse landed on that side.

Long rolled over, trying to catch his breath. He caught a glimpse of Morgan, staring straight ahead.

Long caught his breath, looking where Morgan was staring. Riders appeared from the trees, rifles in hand.

Jacob Keith leading the way, one of the twins next to him. Long got his feet, keeping his hand away from his gun.

"Good idea, marshal. We wouldn't want to kill you before we have our fun," Keith said, reining up.

"Where's the other one, Goren?" Keith said, dismounting.

He motioned for Morgan to do the same. There were too many rifles pointing at him for him to refuse. Morgan slowly stepped from the saddle.

"We sent him back," Long said.

Keith hit Long in the face. Hard, unexpected. Long fell to the ground. Keith kneeled beside him, then laughed.

LAWMAN

"Goren didn't ride for me long, but I doubt he would go back. No, he's probably laying out there somewhere dying. Only kind thing to do as I see it, is go find him, and kill him."

Keith stood then motioned to one of his men, who rode off backtracking the trail Long and Morgan had taken.

Long got to his feet, rubbing his jaw. Keith stared at him, then said,

"Told you to stay off Purple K range. Now, you'll never leave here."

One of the men hit Morgan in the head knocking him down. Before Long could protest, someone hit him. He felt the pain, as he fell to the ground the world went dark.

51

Keith led the men back to the base camp on the large hill. He was feeling good, like a young man again. He had defended his range from invaders just like the old days.

Granted, one of his men had made a terrible decision when he kidnapped that woman. But he would deal with that later. Right now, he had other plans to show the world that the Purple K outfit was still a force to take seriously.

Their arrival at camp was almost at the same time as Buck and Ted's arrival with the woman. She rode in front of Ted, her dress torn, muddy, and stained.

Ted threw her from the saddle onto the ground. She landed hard, screaming in pain. Keith kicked her in the ribs to knock the breath from her.

"Shut up," he said.

She gasped for air, her lungs on fire, her ribs exploding with pain.

Ted dismounted, looked at the woman and said,

"She stinks awful."

Keith looked around. Two of his men were dragging the younger lawman from the saddle he was draped over.

"Tie him to that tree," he said motioning to a tree nearby. "Tie her to that one over there," he motioned to a different tree.

LAWMAN

Ned dropped the lawmen's guns on the ground by the camp.

"What about that one?" he said.

Keith looked over at Long, still unconscious over his saddle.

"I got plans for that one," he said.

He walked over to the tree the woman was tied to as his man tied the last knot in the rope. He looked down at her, then spat in her face.

"All this trouble over you, wench."

Clara flinched as the spit hit her face but still looked from the two men who looked alike.

Staring at the one, she said,

"You killed my friend and took me."

Keith glanced back at Ned, then back at her.

"Ned, that's his name. The other is his twin brother, Ted. Ned didn't kill your friend. Seems he was harder to kill than most or Ned got sloppy. Either way, he's wounded out there. But he will be dead shortly."

Clara stared at the older man, swallowed then said,

"You tell me their names?"

"Oh yeah, why not? I'm Jacob Keith, owner of the Purple K. And you won't live long enough for names to matter no how."

Clara made no reply. A single gunshot pierced the silence, then another. Then nothing.

"Your friend is dead now, whore," Keith said.

Tears rolled from Clara's eyes. She couldn't stop them. She lowered her head so the men wouldn't see her crying.

"Cry all you want but if you make noise, you'll get another kick," Keith said, walking away.

52

His arms hurt, a terrible pain running through his shoulders. That was Long's first thought as he slowly came awake. He tried lowering his arms.

Something held them in place. Above his head. When he looked up the pain in his head intensified. He saw why he couldn't move his arms.

His right arm was tied at the wrist, the rope leading to a tree limb where the rope was pulled tight and tied off. The left was tied the same way, only to a different limb.

He was barely able to touch the ground with the tips of his toes because he was tied up so tight and stretched. His boots were off, he could feel the dirt with his toes.

As he became aware of his situation the pain hit hard. His legs straining to touch the ground, his arms holding his weight, his head with the dull ache.

He looked around the camp. The men sat around the fire talking and laughing amongst themselves.

He glanced to his left. Morgan and Miss Whitney were tied to different trees. Each tied where they were held in place by the ropes, their feet not touching the ground at all. Clara seemed to be struggling with her ropes. Morgan's head was hung low. Long couldn't see if he was breathing.

A man Long didn't know walked up to him. He stared at Long a moment. The punch drove the air from his lungs. The man laughed at having caught the lawman unaware.

"Get the boss. The man is awake."

He hit Long once more then walked off laughing to himself.

Long's toes dug into the dirt trying to find solid footing to give relief to his arms and catch his breath. There was no relief.

Jacob Keith walked up to him, Buck following behind. Buck punched him in the ribs one time. Long gasped from the pain but made no other sound.

"You're tougher stock than your deputy it seems," Keith said, nodding toward Morgan. "He made all kinds of noise when he was hit."

Long looked over at Morgan. He saw Clara looking at him with sympathy and fear. He didn't want to see that; he didn't look back.

"Levi Goren is dead, too. My man got him where you left him. They'll bring him here in a moment."

Long swallowed, then speaking slowly he said,

"You'll kill us three now?"

"Sure enough. Them two first, you I plan on taking my time with. Since you didn't heed my first warning."

"Yeah, sorry about that."

Keith laughed. Buck punched Long in the face causing Long to swing from the ropes on his arms, fire raced along his shoulders to his ribs and legs. He tried to stop the swinging, which would ease the pain, but he couldn't grab enough ground with his toes.

"Don't worry about it, Long. Mistakes happen," Keith said as he walked away, Buck following behind him.

53

It was a damn fool idea taking the dead man back to camp. It was not the first time he had cussed himself for doing it. The horse didn't like the smell of blood that came from the two bullet wounds he had put in the man.

Truth be told, he wasn't used to hauling dead men either. But if Keith wanted a dead man in camp, Levi Goren wasn't one to disappoint.

He had heard the horse approach. Long had left him his pistol, which he used to kill the rider when he first rode up. He thought Goren was dead. He was wrong.

Now they rode along the trail as the last of the sun set behind the rise. It would be full dark in a little while.

Levi had crawled and climbed to reach his horse. Taking more time than he wanted to think about, he had loaded the dead man on the horse he had fell from.

His shoulder bleeding, he made a little mud from the canteen water and stuffed mud into the wound. Now he was riding for a camp not knowing where it was.

He rode on, slumped in the saddle. He smelled wood smoke. Ahead, just the way he was riding.

He saw a glimmer of a campfire. A moan escaped him when he saw how far up the rise the camp was.

He smelled the coffee and food cooking. He realized he was hungrier than he had ever been in his life. He couldn't just ride into camp. Not like this. He decided to take the long way around.

He sat up a little straighter and spurred the horse along, the dead man's horse and the dead man followed without protest.

Levi saw shadows moving about a hundred yards ahead. He quickly dodged into the trees, pulling the extra horse close to him to keep it from nickering.

He sat in the shadows of the trees off the trail a good clip and watched as a group of riders rode past. The distance was too far for him to see who it was or to get an accurate count.

He sat there another ten minutes by the clock in his head after the riders rode past. He eased from the trees to the trail once more.

It was completely dark now. Only a fool would ride in unfamiliar territory in total darkness. But he figured the other two were in trouble. Even if they were all right, Clara was not. The thought of her spurred him on, which caused him to spur the horse onward.

After another hour or so of riding he came to the backside of the camp. He looked at it from the cover of brush and darkness. What he saw shocked him.

One man, maybe Long, was tied to two tree limbs. His back was to him, and Levi could only see what the campfire lit up, which was not much.

Two figures were tied to trees. Not just tied to trees, tied to the middle of the tree trunks. He recognized Clara.

RONNIE ASHMORE

He had the urge to go to her. He fought it down, there would be time. He needed caution from here on out.

54

Long hung there in the middle of two trees. Every muscle in his body was aching and sweat pouring from his forehead into his eyes. He watched the men at the camp.

He had seen them talk amongst themselves, then Keith and a few others, including one of the twins, rode out. He didn't know what that meant.

The pain in his arms was like a constant fire. The burning was intense, and he noticed he had lost feeling in his hands. It hurt to move even his head. His feet were now dangling almost freely, his toes had scraped the ground to the point he had no toe hold to even try to reach anymore.

Now, he felt a sense of dread coming over him. He was tied up and at the mercy of these men, Morgan was tied to his own tree along with Clara at a different tree.

He dared not look in their direction, partly because of the fear he had about what was to come.

A man roused from his sleep, pulled his boots on, then came over to where Clara was tied, her head hanging low on her chest. It was one of the twins, Long saw as he passed by.

He looked down at Clara, then kicked her hard in the leg. As she looked up, the man undid his trousers and relieved himself onto Clara.

RONNIE ASHMORE

She screamed, but quickly quieted as she turned her head away from the bodily fluid that soaked her. She began sobbing quietly, enduring the assault.

Long watched as the insult started.

"Damn you, for that," he said.

The man finished his business, buttoned his trousers, then walked over to Long.

"Don't worry about her, marshal. We got plans for her."

"Which of the twins are you?"

"Ted. Ned went with the others."

Long glanced at Clara, crying and shaking her head. She was soaked from the man's urine. She took a deep breath.

"I hope I see you die for all the atrocities you have done to me," she said, looking at Ted.

Ted looked back at her laughing.

"Ma'am, you and these two ain't long for livin'. When the boys get back, we will finish what we started."

"Back from where?" Long said, trying to shift Ted's focus off Clara.

"Leonville, of course. Mr. Keith figures with all the law out here tied up, so to speak, the town is ripe for pickin'."

A new fear swept over Long.

"Pickin'?"

"Yeah, we are fixing to clean your town out."

Ted walked away laughing. Clara looked over at Long, who was unable to return her look.

Morgan tried shifting his position as he had watched the whole exchange silently.

"What do we do now? Sun will be up in a couple of hours," he said.

Long had no answers.

55

Levi watched from the brush, he saw the whole thing, and heard what Ted had said. As weak as he felt, he knew the three's survival counted on him making a move. But what move? He was grasping for ideas.

Walking quietly to where the horses were tied, the dead man still draped over his saddle, he leaned against his horse and tried to think.

He had a knife and a couple of weapons. His own pistol and rifle along with the dead man's guns.

The rifles he dismissed handily. The recoil would be too much for his wounds to handle.

There were five guys in camp, including Ted. Who was worth another two men at least. Levi checked the loads in his pistol then grabbed the pistol from the dead man's holster. If he did this fast and made every shot count, he might have a chance. Maybe.

Ted would have to die first. That was only proper. He was the most dangerous of the men in the camp. Kill Ted, then worry about the others.

They were still asleep except for Ted, who was stoking the fire back to life. It needed to be done now.

Levi untied the reins of the dead man's horse from the limb. Stroking his face so the horse wouldn't nicker, he led him as far as he dared.

LAWMAN

Levi, a pistol in each hand, took a deep breath, then slapped the horse on the rump with the barrel of one of the pistols.

The horse bolted forward, neighing as it went. It ran straight toward the fire as Levi hoped it would.

Ted, squatting by the fire, was caught unawares. The noise of the horse crashing through the brush made him jump to his feet. He saw nothing except the horse.

The animal and its load ran through the fire scattering ashes and logs all around. Ted drew his pistol, turned to follow the horse's path, then fired at the rider on the horse.

He realized the man was tied to the horse. He knew instantly he was too late. He spun to face the direction the horse had come from.

Levi stepped out into the clearing as Ted turned. Levi fired three times from his right-hand pistol. Levi saw the bullets hit home, saw Ted stagger, then fall.

Levi had no time to make sure Ted was dead. Others had jumped up at the noise and gunfire.

Using both pistols, Levi fired at each man as he saw movement. Each shot finding a target and causing men to cry out or die instantly.

When the threats were gone, Levi walked over to a wounded Ted. He looked down at the man. Two of his bullets hit him in the stomach. The man was gritting his teeth in pain.

"To hell with you, traitor," Ted said.

Levi cocked his pistol and aimed it at Ted's head, then smiled. He holstered the pistol, kicked Ted's gun out of reach and walked off.

56

Long watched all the action along with Morgan and Clara. Levi walked to him, knife in hand, and began cutting the rope on his right hand.

"Looks painful."

Long stayed silent, his right arm dropped helplessly to his side as the rope was cut. His body dropped over causing pain in the left arm. Levi cut the other rope and Long fell to the ground.

He landed hard, his hands and arms not able to break his fall. He lay on the ground groaning, rolling to his back. He watched as Levi went to Clara and cut her ropes.

"They said you were dead."

"Nearly am, it seems. Are you OK?"

As he helped Clara to her feet, he hugged her, tightly. Clara started crying, Levi held his back, almost.

Clara's dress was still wet from Ted's disgusting act. She back away from Levi, and said,

"I'm a mess. That man..."

"Can't hurt you anymore. I won't let nothing hurt you ever again. I promise."

"You gonna cut me loose or what?"

Levi glanced at Morgan, then began cutting his ropes. As he cut, he said,

"You left me out there. They came for me. I was near helpless out there. I didn't know you were prisoners until I came up here to see if Clara was here."

"Thanks for coming."

Levi stopped cutting. He pointed the knife at Morgan, then said,

"I didn't come for you. I came for her. If I could have got her and left you, I believe I would have."

Long managed to get to his knees. He still couldn't raise his arms. The tingling from the blood flowing back to them was painful.

"Who's missing from over there?"

Levi finished freeing Morgan. Then walked over to the campfire to count the dead. All were dead, including Ted. He looked back at Long, who was trying to stand up.

Feeling weak, Levi sat down. His shoulder throbbed, and his side hurt. Clara came to his side and knelt to check his wounds. "Ned, Buck, and Keith. Two or three others. That's who I saw ride out, I guess."

Long staggered to his feet, Morgan helping him balance.

"They went to town. That's what Ted said. When they came back, they were going to kill us."

"Joke's on them, huh. We are bruised and battered but still kickin'," Morgan said, helping Long to sit beside Levi and Clara. "I'll go saddle some horses and find some guns."

LAWMAN

Clara looked over at Long, then at Levi. "I'm afraid I'm not much of a lady right now. I stink and look a wreck. But I am glad you all came for me."

"You're more of a lady than this cowboy deserves to even look at Clara."

She looked at Levi, blushing.

57

"I think this is a bad idea, boss."

The men sat their horses at the edge of town watching and planning. Sunup would be in a few minutes. The plan had been discussed at length on the ride in.

"We talked about this, Buck. We clean out the town, we get back to our camp by dark and we kill the prisoners."

"That's what I mean. Couldn't we have killed them before we left?"

Keith shook his head in disgust.

"You're acting like an old woman. Now, we show this town we are the force to deal with. Hell, there used to that because of Ritter and his doings."

"Seem to recall he's dead."

Keith looked at his foreman hard.

"My ranch, my say. Understood?"

Buck nodded.

"We going to the saloon first?" Ned asked, hoping to get the raid started.

"We will be going everywhere. Each business and house will give over their money and anything we decide to take."

"What about resistance?" one of the newer men asked.

LAWMAN

Keith couldn't remember his name. Todd? Bob? He just couldn't remember.

"Tom," Ned said, "If they resist, we shoot 'em. Right, boss?"

Tom. That was his name. Keith nodded.

"That's right, Tom. Shoot 'em."

Buck shifted his weight in the saddle. He looked over the town once more as the sun started to rise. The morning sun chased the darkness of night away.

"All right. We go to the saloon first. We kick our way in. Each of you can have one drink. Then you fan out and start with the houses. The businesses will be last. Understood?" Buck said, pushing his horse forward.

The rest followed behind. Keith felt annoyed with his foreman. He made a note to talk to him later.

At the saloon, they were surprised to see it was already opened. The bartender was standing on the boardwalk as they reined up in front of the building.

"Kinda early for a bar to be opened, ain't it?" Keith said as he watched the bartender.

"Not at all, Mr. Keith. We open for breakfast. You boys hungry?"

The bartender turned and walked back inside. Keith looked around the town again. No one seemed to be paying them any mind.

"I'm hungry. Let's eat," Ned said, dismounting.

The rest of the men followed Ned inside. Buck and Keith stood on the boardwalk looking around.

"I don't like this, boss. We should stick to the plan."

"Food never hurt nobody. Let's eat now, then tear the place up."

Keith walked into the bar telling himself he needed to have a talk with Buck soon. [OBJ]

58

Frannie sat on her porch, hidden by the bushes in her yard. She watched as Silas had talked to the men, then they all went inside.

Martha Ritter came from inside the house. Frannie had enjoyed her company last night as they had sat and talked about all kinds of things, especially Jim Long.

"Anything?" Martha asked, handing Frannie a cup of coffee.

"Those awful men are in town just like the mayor said they'd be."

"I'm surprised they are here."

"What does that mean for Jim and Morgan?" Frannie asked, looking up at Martha.

"No telling. I just can't rightfully say."

Frannie felt a pang of fear grip her insides, cold, harsh. If those men were in town and Jim wasn't that could only mean one thing, at least to Frannie. Jim Long lay dead out there somewhere on the prairie.

She fought back the tears she felt forming. She had to be strong, at least for Martha. It was her two sons after all.

"Could be they missed each other out there on the trail with the boys looking for Miss Whitney."

RONNIE ASHMORE

Frannie decided at once that was it. They were fine, Jim was fine. She would hold onto that for now.

A knock on the door frame from inside the house startled both women. They turned as one and looked back.

Mayor Tomey was coming from the house. He closed the door gently, then said,

"I apologize for sneaking in like this. I wanted to avoid the street as much as possible. I see they are at the saloon already."

Tomey was dressed in rough clothes, not his usual everyday dress. Frannie could not recall seeing him in rough clothes before.

"Just like you said. They are here and Jim and Morgan aren't," Frannie said.

"Well, Jim and Morg had a wounded man to look after too. I'm sure that is slowing them down," Tomey said.

"That's true," she said, as if she had been thinking the same thing. Martha placed a hand on her shoulder.

"This town is tough. It can handle whatever a handful of hateful men can dish out," Martha said.

"It's been through worse, that's a fact," Frannie said.

"Yeah, but this time, the town has learned a lesson or two. Thanks to your son, Martha. I think we will be ready for whatever happens."

"When will it happen?" Martha said.

LAWMAN

"Whenever Silas gets done feeding them. Come on, we need to go," Frannie said, standing up and leading everyone in the house.

59

Long watched as dawn slowly came to the rise. He still couldn't move his arms well, the pain was getting less, but the soreness was awful. He constantly moved his arms whenever he could.

Clara and Morgan had gathered all the dead men's weapons. Rifles, pistols, knifes, they were all piled in the middle and the men took what they wanted. Clara chose a knife. A long blade, bone handled knife.

She caught Morgan's look as she hefted it in her hand.

"I don't aim to be taken prisoner again."

Long chuckled, Levi and Morgan shook their heads.

"What is the plan for town?" Morgan said, saddling a horse for Clara.

He had already saddled everyone else's horse. He was eager to get on the trail and back to town.

"We need to study the layout and see what they are doing. Go from there, I guess," Long said.

"Clara, once all this mess is over and we are back in town, I aim to marry you. If you'll have me."

Clara looked at Levi speechless for a moment. Finally, she said,

LAWMAN

"Marry me? Why in the world would you want to marry me? I'm useless to any man right now. I'm hardly a proper lady."

Levi felt like a fool. He stood in front of her feeling naked as the day he was born. He wanted to take the words back, not because he didn't mean them. But because all eyes were on him now. He swallowed and tried to smile. He had jumped in the creek; he might as well see if he could swim.

"Ma'am, Clara. I have no right asking a lady like you to marry a man such as me. I'm a fiddle-footed drifter, a saddle bum, and a man who never thought a woman was made for him. But I believe you are, Clara. I'll get a store job if it means being with you..."

She placed a hand on his chest interrupting him.

"Levi, I can't see you in an apron tending a store and being a store clerk."

Morgan laughed, then seeing the look from Long, he stifled it.

Clara ignored Morgan as she continued.

"I have never met a more honorable and sweeter man than you, though. While I can't see the clerk part, I can see the marriage part. I'd be honored to be your wife."

Morgan smiled, then looked over at Long. Long ignored the look and stepped into the saddle, slowly.

"Before anyone marries anyone, we have a town to see to."

RONNIE ASHMORE

He spurred his horse, not waiting for the others. They would catch up.

60

Ned and the boys took advantage of a breakfast they had no intention of paying for. After several helpings of flapjacks, steak, and eggs with bacon, along with three pots of coffee, they all sat back in their chairs feeling content.

Except Buck. He and Keith had eaten their share, but Buck was uneasy. Keith could see that as he constantly looked out the only window in the saloon.

"What's bugging you, boy?"

Buck looked at Keith. His beard was stained with tobacco, and unkempt. His hair looked as if it hadn't been combed out in years. Sometimes, even after all these years, it was hard to have faith in a man like this.

Buck leaned in, speaking softly.

"I don't know. I feel we should have stuck to our plan. Back at camp. Taking care of that, not venturing out here."

"Think of this as a gift. The whole town is opened to us because those lawmen are tied up at camp."

Buck sat back in his chair, ran his hands through his hair, then nodded.

"OK. If you say so."

"I say so," Keith said, sipping his coffee.

RONNIE ASHMORE

Silas brought more coffee to the table to refill the cups. Keith waved him off. Silas returned the pot and stood at the bar.

Keith and his men all stood in unison. Keith looked over at Silas.

"Thanks for breakfast."

"No problem. I'll just put this on your tab."

"Tab?"

"Yes, sir. You and your men have been coming in so often I figured it would be easier to run a tab."

Keith looked over at Buck, then shrugged a shoulder.

"Sure. We will be back for the whiskey in a while."

"Yes, sir. Enjoy your time in town," Silas said, going to the back of the bar to the storeroom.

Buck led the men outside to their horses. When they were mounted, Keith looked at them and said,

"All right, we go to the houses first then the businesses."

The men nodded and mumbled their agreements. Keith was feeling good when they rode down a side street to the first house. They reined up in front of it.

Keith motioned for Tom to go knock on the door. Tom dismounted and walked toward the small frame house that needed paint and carpentry work.

LAWMAN

"What are we gonna take from this place?" Tom asked as he walked by Keith and Buck.

"Despite it looking like a hog pen, whatever we get is more than we had," Keith said.

Tom knocked on the door.

61

Standing on the roof of the hotel, Mayor Tomey watched the men mount up, talk amongst themselves a moment, then ride to the nearest house.

Keeping below the roof line of the building, he and one of Martha Ritter's ranch hands watched as one man dismounted and walked to the door.

Tomey looked over at the hand.

"All the men are in place?"

The hand nodded, then said,

"The women are in the hotel as you wanted."

"Hopefully Long and them will be back before the shooting starts."

The man held his hat in his hands to avoid being seen by the Purple K men. He rubbed sweat from his face with his free hand.

"Mayor, me and the rest of the boys are here as a favor to Mrs. Ritter. But we ain't no gun fighters, we are cow men. If it comes to shootin', you may be alone."

Tomey nodded, still watching the men.

"What's your name?"

"J.R."

"Well, J.R. Hopefully if there is shooting the men in the houses can take care of it."

"You planned all this out, huh?"

"As much as I could. The women and children in the hotel..."

Tomey stopped talking as he watched the rider kick at the door to the house. It was a ramshackle house.

The door splintered at the same moment a shotgun blast sounded from inside. The rider was hit full force by the shotgun blast as he was preparing to kick the door again.

He flew back, falling to the ground as rifle shots came from inside. Other shots were coming from other houses, as the men came from inside their own houses and joined the fight.

Men started yelling, horses started bucking and rearing. One man was thrown from his horse. He stood, drawing his pistol. His head exploded as the bullet of an unknown sniper found his target.

Tomey was excited to see his plan working. It had been his idea to set a trap in case the Purple K riders came to town.

The folks had objected at first, then Martha Ritter had talked all of them into going along. Now, watching the scene below, he made a mental note that he owed her one.

RONNIE ASHMORE

Keith started yelling, and the others started running for cover, trying to get away from the gun fire that had killed two of them before they knew they were in a fight.

"Fall back," Keith yelled. "Seek cover, boys."

One man, who was covered in blood, spurred his horse hard heading out of town to the south. Tomey watched him ride away, never looking back.

The three remaining men scattered on foot, leaving their horses behind.

"Go down and tell them to be on the lookout."

J.R. left without a word.

62

Hearing the gunfire before they could see the town, Long and the rest reined up, listening.

"Sounds like a war down there," Morgan said.

"We might be too late, Jim."

Long considered what Levi said. It may well be too late. Clara stared out at the landscape, seeing nothing.

"Too much killing out here. Just too much."

"It ain't always like this, ma'am."

"Oh, Morgan, I know you think this is normal. But it's not."

"You having second thoughts on settling in this country, ma'am?"

Clara looked from Morgan to Levi. She felt so out of place in this country. But she knew she loved the injured man who was looking back at her. She shook her head.

"No, just the law needs to do a better job of keeping ruffians away."

Long shook his head, then said,

"We are trying."

"How do you want to play this?"

"We need to get to town without being shot for the enemy."

Levi grunted, then spat.

"Don't mean to be a nuisance. But I need a doctor soon."

Long considered the options for a moment, picturing the town in his mind. At last, he said,

"OK. We go for the livery first. Then Levi, work your way to the doctor's office."

"That's it?" Morgan said.

"For now."

Long spurred his horse and led the way

down the hill toward the town. The sounds of gun shots were louder and closer together than before.

Long tried to form a plan in his mind as he rode. Without seeing what was happening it was impossible to plan any course of action.

The livery might not be safe by the time they rode into town. He had no second option of where to go.

Levi needed the doctor, that was more important than anything at the moment. He looked bad when he had ridden into camp and saved their lives, he was looking worse now.

Long raised one arm and rolled the shoulder, then the other. The pain was still there, but he could move each of them well enough. His wrists were chaffed where he had been hanging from them. He flexed his fingers as he rode.

"What are you thinking?"

LAWMAN

Long looked at Morgan, then shook his head.

"Thinking how much I hate this job. I was much happier not being a lawman than I ever knew at the time."

Morgan didn't respond. They could see the town and men standing in the streets shooting.

63

Jacob Keith and Buck took cover behind an old wagon near the opening of the street that they had ridden down. Keith looked around for Ned, he didn't see the man anywhere.

It had turned into a bloodbath. Two of his men shot down without warning, one coward had turned tail and rode out. Good riddance to him anyway.

The horses had taken off the first chance they had once the men dismounted. They were nowhere to be seen either.

Buck snapped a shot at a man in the street, he fell not moving.

"This ain't good."

"No kidding. Just kill who you can."

Keith fired two shots at a man was coming to the aid of the fallen man in the street. He staggered, then fell beside the first man. He didn't move again.

Sounds of running came from behind them. Both men turned to shoot, they held their fire when they saw Ned, pistol in hand, running bent over to join them.

Ned stopped beside Buck and motioned behind him.

"That marshal is comin', along with three others."

Ned saw the look that passed between Keith and Buck.

LAWMAN

"Why are they free?" he asked, ducking as a bullet hit the wood beside him.

Ned fired a shot back, not seeing if he hit anything.

"These people were ready for us. We need to get out of here now."

Keith nodded at Buck's words but said nothing. He cursed himself silently. Why didn't he listen to his foreman.

"The boys are probably trailin' the marshal now. We may have help comin'."

Buck stared at the gunman, Keith said what they both knew.

"Help ain't coming, son. The boys are dead or dying back there on that hill."

"We need horses," Buck said.

Ned fired another shot into the unknown, then said,

"Come on."

He led the other two back the way he had come. They headed down the alley between two houses, neither had windows that looked out that way.

Behind the businesses along this side of town there were no men stationed. Keith was surprised to see no one pursuing them from the other street.

The shooting had stopped. The horses were standing wide eyed in the middle of the main street.

RONNIE ASHMORE

The men ran to their horses. As they stepped into the saddle, a shotgun boomed from somewhere behind them. Buck's chest blew apart as the buckshot hit him in the back, throwing him from the saddle.

Ned turned and returned fire toward the saloon, driving Silas back inside before he could fire the second barrel.

Keith fired toward the marshal and the group riding toward town, knowing the range was too far for his pistol.

"Let's get out of here," Keith said, spurring his horse and leaving dust in his path. Ned rode beside him, not saying anything.

64

Long saw the men saddle up, saw Silas empty one saddle, the shot fired in their direction was too far to worry about. He kept going.

Morgan pointed. Long saw what he was looking at and led the group to the hotel. About twenty men were standing, grinning, and looking at each other with the look men give when they survive what they thought would kill them.

Women came from the hotel to stand on the porch. Long saw Frannie and his mother among the crowd. The doctor pushed through to meet the group as they reined up.

"Get him to my office, now," he said, pointing at Morgan.

Morgan and Clara led Levi toward the doctor's office.

Long stepped from the saddle, gently. Frannie was in his arms instantly. Long felt a moment of embarrassment to be carrying on like this in public. He hugged her just as hard as she was hugging him.

"We thought you dead," she said when she finally broke the embrace.

"What happened here?" he said, looking around.

"Mayor Tomey," someone next to him said, as if that explained it.

Long looked at Frannie, who smiled, and said,

RONNIE ASHMORE

"The mayor figured you and Morgan were dead. He planned this in case the Purple K riders came to town. The women and children at the hotel, the men armed in the houses and stores. Folks thought him crazy..."

"Crazy like a fox," Long said, looking for the mayor.

Martha came to stand beside Long and gave him a hug.

"I knew you were OK," she said.

Long laughed.

"How's Levi and Ms. Whitney?" Martha said.

"Levi is hurt. Ms. Whitney isn't injured but I'm guessing she's hurt too. Morg is with them."

"Marshal, we got dead of our own out here, too," someone said from the street.

Long walked over to where the dead men were laying in the middle of the street.

Long recognized one of the men laying on his back as a local who never said much to anyone. He knelt, rolling the other one over to his back. One of the men in the crowd swore, a few women gasped, including his mother. He vaguely heard the noise. He stood, staring at Mayor Tomey's lifeless body.

"My Lord," Martha said. "Mayor Tomey was the reason we all fought those men off."

Long pushed his hat back on his head, then looked around and pointed to a couple of men.

LAWMAN

"Get him off the street. See to it he's taken care of properly."

Long pushed his way past the crowd. He walked to his office. He was tired, he wanted sleep and food. But he needed to think.

65

In the small room that served as the operating room in Doctor Neils small office, Clara stood out of the way watching Neils work on Levi's shoulder. He tried to be still but grimaced in pain as the doctor worked.

The room was stuffy and cramped. She should have waited with Morgan in the other room, but she dismissed that thought.

Levi had said he wanted to marry her; she had said she would marry him. Life had taken an unexpected turn. She had never really known what love was. She was confident she loved Levi and he loved her.

She still wore her tattered and stained clothes. The smell of stale sweat and urine, both hers and that other man's, was strong in the air. If the doctor noticed he didn't say anything.

Morgan opened the door after a light tap.

"Ma'am, Frannie and Mrs. Ritter are here to see you."

Clara looked at Morgan, panic in her eyes. She rubbed her hands down her dress unknowingly. She followed Morgan into the small waiting room. Morgan took his leave and left the office.

Frannie gave her a hug, which shocked Clara. Mrs. Ritter patted her on the shoulder, smiling.

"I'm so happy to see you are all right," Frannie said, breaking the hug.

LAWMAN

Clara, aware of how she smelled, said,

"I'm just glad to be found and that everyone is OK."

"We lost two townsfolk in that fighting earlier. Mayor Tomey was one of them," Martha said.

Clara looked from one woman to the other. She felt tears welling in her eyes. She was unable to stop them from rolling down her cheek.

"Such a sweet man. Dead because of me. I'm so sorry..."

Martha hugged Clara, then said,

"A sweet man, yes. Dead because of you, no, not at all. The men responsible for this mess paid the price. Two got away, I hear."

Martha released the embrace. Frannie pat her back, and said,

"Clara, if I may call you that, let's get you cleaned and freshened up a bit."

"I can't leave Levi alone."

"Levi is in good hands. Besides you'll feel better after bath and clean clothes and some food," Martha said.

"I guess I do look a fright and smell worse."

"On the way you can tell us all about the wedding "

Clara looked at Frannie, surprised. Martha laughed a little as they all went out the door.

RONNIE ASHMORE

"I should tell you now, my son, Morgan, has a mouth that can't keep a secret."

"I'll remember that."

The ladies walked toward the hotel. Clara was doubtful she would ever be clean again.

66

Keith and Ned reined up at a small creek. The horses drank deep, blowing and drinking more. Ned patted his sweat soaked horse and looked at their backtrail.

"I don't think they are chasing us."

"Why would they? They wiped out our whole gang. Just you and me now, Ned."

"You think the boys in camp are dead?"

Keith looked at his young enforcer.

"You know of any other reason those four would come riding into town pretty as you please?"

"Sir, that means Ted is dead. Don't it?"

"Every one of them, son."

Keith led his horse from the creek, he started adjusting his cinch.

"What now? When do we go back?"

"Back? We ain't going back. We ain't going to the ranch or anywhere else we can be found."

"You mean we're just gonna run?"

"For now, until we regroup."

Ned considered Keith's words. He shook his head not liking any of it.

RONNIE ASHMORE

"We don't need to regroup. We need to go kill that marshal and his deputy."

"You're being foolish talking like that. They'd be waiting for you to ride in just like they waited for us."

"Seems to me, boss this was your idea. Sacking the town and all. We should have handled business at camp."

Keith walked away a few feet. He ran his fingers through his hair, put his hat back on, then said,

"I messed up. It cost me my whole crew. Some of them men had been with me for years. Like Buck and your brother. What do you want me to do?"

"I want to see the camp. I want to bury my brother."

"If they come looking for us, that will be the first place they start. It's too dangerous. Our best play is to ride on somewhere else, let things die down, then come back with a new crew."

"A new crew? Where do you think you will find men more loyal than Buck and Ted were? No, I'm going to look at the camp. I'm burying my brother. Then I'm killin' that marshal and all his friends."

Keith turned to face Ned, looking him in the eye. They were within feet of each other.

"You'll do nothing of the sort. You still ride for me, and I'm still the K in the Purple K, in case you forgot, son."

Ned returned the stare.

LAWMAN

"I'm not your son. And there is no Purple K anymore," he slipped the thong from his pistol.

"You gonna draw on me, boy. I took you in when you were a pup. You want to kill me now?"

"I wanted to marry that woman. I wanted to leave the country with her and live a life. You wouldn't let me. You had to have your way."

"I ain't drawing on you, son."

Ned took a step closer to Keith, who tried to back up. Ned drew his pistol and shot Keith in the forehead. The bullet left a little third eye in the center of the man's head but blew brains and bone out the back of his head.

Ned holstered his gun, took a deep breath, and looked down at Keith for a moment. He gathered both horses and remounted. He rode off toward the Purple K without looking back.

67

Ned rode into the camp on the rise as the sun was sinking beneath the hills. He dismounted and walked slowly through the campsite. The smell of death was strong on the rise. The men had met a sudden and violent end.

The dead men were bloated and had turned colors in death. Ned found his brother lying by the cold campfire. He was lying on his side. Flies were buzzing around his eyes and opened mouth.

Ned shewed them away with his hat. The tears came unexpectedly, blurring his vision, rolling down his cheeks. He couldn't remember the last time he hd cried. He let the tears flow.

He kneeled beside his brother. He tried to close Ted's mouth, but it kept coming open, flies kept trying to get inside. Ted's eyes refused to stay closed, no matter how many times Ned closed them.

Thoughts flooded Ned's mind as he cried over his brother. Mr. Keith finding both boys alone on the street in Austin after being abandoned by their parents, how Jacob Keith had taken them in, raised them. Buck was already at the ranch then, a young man, but seemed old to the boys.

The twins had killed for the first time when they were fourteen. A Mexican drifter who happened to be crossing Purple K range without knowing. Keith had made the boys take turns shooting the man until he died. Then celebrated that night. From then on it was robbing, rustling, and killing. All in the name of the brand.

When the tears stopped, Ned stood. He wiped his face and put his hat on. He looked around the camp, then down at his brother.

"Brother, I'd like to give you a buryin'. I really would. But it's dark soon, I don't have a shovel, and I don't guess it would do much good to bury you and say Bible words over you anyway. We both know you're dancing with the ol' devil as we speak."

Ned went to his horse, stepped into the saddle, and leading the extra horse Keith had ridden, rode out of camp down the hill.

He was thinking he ought to feel something, pain, anger, remorse. He only felt determined.

He slumped in the saddle as he rode. He needed rest for now. He could plan his next move after a meal and a night's sleep.

68

Long stood in the street listening to the people talk. Men and women seemed to be standing around talking in high voices. Everyone was talking at once, wanting to be heard, wanting their opinion to count. Long wasn't interested in hearing any of it.

He was tired, he ached all over his body, and he wanted sleep. He tried to walk away from the crowd by going through the mob of people. A man stepped into his path blocking his way.

"What are you gonna do about the two that got away?"

Long looked at the man, then cast a glance at the crowd.

"Nothing."

The crowd erupted with groans as Long suspected they would. He heard the men swear as he stood looking at them.

"Look. Hush down," he said. The crowd quieted, he continued, "We had a bad time, no doubt. Our teacher kidnapped, a man shot down, and a town attacked. But the teacher is safe, the wounded man is over at Dr. Neil's resting, and you good people defended our town..."

"Our mayor is dead," a voice shouted in the back. The crowd got loud again.

"I know. But the reason is because I and my deputy left to find the teacher, Ms. Whitney. I will not leave the town unprotected again."

LAWMAN

A man stepped up to the front of the crowd. He was a man Long knew but couldn't place his name. He said,

"Marshal, what if you deputize some of us to go looking for those two that got away."

"You want to risk going after those two, go ahead. As far as I'm concerned until they ride back into this town, I have no reason to go looking for them."

Long pushed his way through the crowd. It would be dark soon; all he wanted was a hot bath and a soft bed.

He walked toward the hotel with the murmurs and voices fading behind him as he went.

He felt a sadness and a little guilty about Mayor Tomey being killed. If he had not gone off maybe it wouldn't have happened. But he had to go search for Ms. Whitney. The sheriff was not going to help, so he had essentially been left alone to do the best he could.

Tomey was a good man. And it rankled something inside Long to let the two men responsible for his death ride out and not pursue.

He stepped on the porch and looked back the way he had come. His obligation was to the town.

He sighed then entered the hotel, not caring what tomorrow would bring.

69

Clara Whitney was surprised to see Marshal Long come into the hotel lobby. She felt clean and refreshed after an hour-long soak in a hot bath. Her dress was a fresh one from her room, and she smelled of lilac perfume.

Frannie, who had been beside her helping her get clean, swore she was as beautiful as ever. Clara didn't think so.

She knew she had bathed in water hot enough to scald, but she swore she could still smell urine and feces and body odor ever now and then.

Frannie's face lit up when she saw the marshal. Clara smiled at him as he walked up.

"Well, Ms. Whitney. I hope you are feeling a little better."

"Yes, sir. I am on my way to see Levi... Mr. Goren. I'd like to see him before it's too late tonight."

Long nodded, then looked at Frannie, who said,

"You look terrible."

He smiled a tired smile.

"The townsfolk aren't happy with me now. I won't go after those two that got away."

Clara shivered a little at the mention of the men who had kidnapped her.

LAWMAN

"I'm not a vengeful person. But I'd like to see them hanged for what they've done."

Frannie patted Clara's arm. A gesture that Clara was unsure of what the intent was.

Clara ignored the pat on the arm and said,

"You aren't going after those men?"

Long shook his head.

"No. I'm not leaving the town unprotected again."

"So, they get away. Is that it?"

Frannie looked at Clara and said,

"Clara, I think what Jim is saying..."

"I know what he's saying. I'm disappointed in what I am hearing. We almost died on that mountain, Mayor Tomey did die, and you just let them go."

Frannie and Long looked at her. She cleared her throat, then said,

"If you'll excuse me. I need to go see Levi."

She pushed past Long and walked out of the hotel.

"She's been through a lot."

"I know, I don't blame her for being mad at me."

"I guess her, and Levi Goren are to be married?"

Long shrugged.

RONNIE ASHMORE

"Do proposals when you're thinking you'll die count?"

Frannie laughed, and said,

"Oh, yeah. They do. So be careful what you say."

She squeezed his arm as she made her way to the door of the hotel. Long watched her go, then went to the desk and ordered a hot bath.

70

The sun streaming through the curtains woke Ned from a death like sleep. He was unsure where he was for a moment. He sat up in the bed, looking around. He was in the main house of the Purple K, in Jacob Keith's room, in his bed.

He smiled as he put his feet on the floor and reached for his clothes. He had never been allowed to sleep in the main house. He and Ted had always, since the first night, slept in the bunkhouse.

He had never been farther inside than the room that served as Keith's office. He dressed, then took advantage of the daylight to look around the house. It was not what he expected.

True, the outside had never looked like much. It seemed to always need repairs, and at times appeared to be barely standing. He and Ted had laid awake at night talking and dreaming of what kind of treasure the inside of the house held.

Ned walked from room to room looking, disappointed at what he saw. The furniture was roughhewn, made from leftover wood and scraps from the ranch. The table in the small dining room was hastily made, one leg shorter than the rest making the table lean to one side. The main room was bare, no decorations, no pictures, nothing that showed that it was a home for all these years.

Ned walked to the office, which was at the front of the house. He searched desk drawers and cabinets looking for anything of value. He only found a little money, about thirty dollars he guessed. He put it in his pocket. He looked around the room again, then walked back through the house.

Not a lot to show for all the years Jacob Keith had lived in the house. All the stealing and killing and taking advantage of other people, in the long run, had not been worth it, it seemed now.

Ned took a coal lamp from the hanger on the wall of the kitchen. He turned and threw it against the wall of the main room. Oil ran down the dirty wall.

He found two lamps in the office. He took them apart, pouring the oil on the floor, making a trail to the front door.

He stood on the porch for a moment, searching his pockets, then shook his head. He went back into the house to the kitchen and found matches.

Back on the porch, he considered what he was planning. He knew this house, like the man who had built it and lived in it, had to go. This was the only house Ned remembered when he thought about his life.

He struck a match with his thumbnail tossing it into the house on the puddle of coal oil by the door.

The liquid caught and the flame leapt to life blazing a trail into the house. Ned stood on the porch, watching to make sure the fire would burn.

LAWMAN

He inhaled deeply, breathing the fumes of coal oil, the char or wood, and the smoke from the fire.

He went to the barn, saddled his horse, then rode out of the yard of the ranch. He didn't look back at the burning house.

71

Long wanted food, he had not eaten since the night before and it was little enough. He looked over at the restaurant as he stepped off the porch of the hotel.

Frannie would be working this morning, but he saw a lot of people around the restaurant this morning. He was in no mood to talk to anyone or to hear opinions on what he should do. His mind was settled.

It was foolish to go chasing after those two men and leave the town defenseless if they came back. Of course, if they did come back and killed him the town would be defenseless for the most part anyway.

At least he would be here, along with Morgan, if they did come back. Though he expected them to lay low and hide for a while. Keith had lost all his men except Ned.

Ned was the one Long wanted to see hanged. But it was silly to go chasing after him when he could be halfway to Mexico by now.

He decided against food and walked to the office instead. As he approached, he saw a man sitting in the chair in front of his office. A wagon was parked in front of the office. Long didn't recognize the man. The man stood as Long approached.

"Marshal, morning to you."

Long nodded, not sure what the man wanted.

LAWMAN

"Sorry to bother you so early, but I need to talk to you."

"Want to come inside, I'll make coffee." The man followed Long into the office and stood staring as Long got the stove going for coffee.

The man was about fifty, dirty clothes that had holes in the knees and his shirt was dirty and worn thin. His hat was floppy and ragged.

"Never been to this town before. Hear'd of it a time or two though."

Long set the coffee pot on the stove, then turned to the man, and said,

"Well, what brings you here this morning, Mr..."

"Name's ain't a concern now, Marshal."

Long poured himself a cup of coffee then offered the man a cup, which he refused. Long sat in his chair.

"What is the concern then mister?"

"Oh, I's coming to town early this morning, not this town but Center. Longer trek for me but I never cottoned to this town much. Anyways, that's when I saw it. That's the concern. The dead man."

Long stood, looked at the man, then said,

"Dead man? Where?"

The stranger stood as well. He nodded toward the door.

"My wagon. That's what I been trying to tell ya."

RONNIE ASHMORE

Long went out to the man's wagon. He looked in the back. Jacob Keith stared sightlessly into the morning sun.

Long looked at the stranger, who only shrugged his shoulders.

72

News of Jacob Keith's death spread fast. Most of the town seemed happy he was dead. Long couldn't blame them for that, but questions kept nagging him.

Why was Keith dead? Where was Ned? Those questions would have to wait. A knock at the door of his office broke his thinking. The door opened slowly.

"Marshal?"

Long stood and came around to open the door the rest of the way letting his visitor in.

"Ms. Whitney. I'm surprised to see you."

"Well, I needed to talk to you, marshal." Long offered her a seat. When she had sat down, she took a deep breath, then said,

"Keith is dead, is that right?"

"Yes, ma'am. Killed along a creek north of here a ways out."

"What about the other one? The one who took me and shot Levi?"

"I don't know where he is. Speaking of Levi, I was going to go see him later. How is he?"

"He's fine, he should be up and around soon."

Clara wanted to say something else, Long could see her trying to decide to say it or not.

"Is there something else, ma'am?"

She smiled a little, then scrunched her shoulders.

"Levi asked me to marry him. I plan to do just that, but I am scared of that man, the one who shot him."

She hesitated a moment.

"That's understandable. You have been through a lot. I hope you and Levi will be happy."

She started to say something in reply, but Morgan came into the office and interrupted whatever she was going to say. She stood, looked at Morgan, then back at Long.

"I've taken enough of your time, Marshal Long. Mr. Ritter, good day."

Morgan closed the door behind her, then said to his brother,

"She sure cleans up nice, don't she?"

Long just looked at Morgan.

"Anyway, I came to tell ya, ma is going to come to town later. She has something to talk to you about and no, I don't know what."

"I wonder where Ned is?"

"Ned? He's probably near Mexico by now."

"I don't know why he'd go there. All his friends and his brother are dead. Killing his boss makes him the last of the Purple K."

LAWMAN

"Good riddance to them. Ranchers will sleep a little easier knowin' that gang of rustlers is out of business," Ned said, stretching in his chair.

"Which leads me back to my original question. Where's Ned?"

73

Long stood quietly with the rest of the town who were crowded around the grave of Mayor Mark Tomey. The preacher talked of his bravery and his leadership of the town. Long couldn't argue with either of the preacher's points.

It was the second funeral of the day for the town. The other man who had died during the attack was buried on his own land with just his widow and the preacher as mourners. A simple man simply buried.

The mayor's funeral showed none of that simplicity. It seemed the whole town had turned out for this, and the preacher wasn't going to waste an opportunity to preach to folks who might not ever set foot in his church. Long wanted to leave but considering where he was standing it would draw too much attention from the other people. An Amen broke into his thoughts as people began filing away.

He turned to walk from the cemetery, Martha and Frannie came up beside him.

"He was a good man," Martha said.

"What will happen now?" Frannie asked.

"The town will elect a new mayor at some point. Who knows who that will be," Long said, avoiding most of the other people heading down the hill to town.

"Too bad a woman can't be mayor," Frannie said.

LAWMAN

"That's silly."

Martha slapped Long's arm lightly.

"Don't say that. Women are as capable as men are. Though Frannie James is right about something. It's silly only because we don't have a say in it."

Long was glad Frannie let the topic drop. His mother could carry on about such things if given a notion.

Clara Whitney joined them at the bottom of the hill. She fell in step with them as they walked.

"How's Levi?" Martha asked.

"Fine, thank you for asking."

"Any word on when school will begin?" Clara looked at Frannie, then said,

"No. Truth to tell, I haven't thought about it."

"Well, it needs some thought, Ms. Whitney," Martha said. "That man we just planted in the ground had high hopes for that school and you. You can't let him down."

Long felt a little sympathy for Clara Whitney, he had seen firsthand what she had been through.

"There will be time for school and electing new mayors and all other things when the town settles back down," he said.

They walked the rest of the way to town in silence.

74

Ned sat cross-legged on the ground. He was on rise overlooking the town. He could see the funeral people gathered at the cemetery, though the distance was too far to make out who was who.

He was hidden by some mesquite limbs and brush, though he wasn't too worried about being seen. He tried to think of a plan and how to get at that marshal down there.

Every plan he considered he dismissed due to the complexity of it. All he had wanted in the beginning was that woman.

She was the prettiest thing he had ever

seen, that was true. But his actions had led to this. She was the reason he had no brother, no friends, and no home. Her and that lawman friend of hers.

He dismissed the woman. Forget her, he had to focus on killing that lawman. He was the reason all this was happening to him.

He took a deep breath. His thoughts were running wild, getting away from him again. He wished Keith were here, he'd know what to do.

But Keith was dead. Ned shook his head to clear his thoughts again. Keith died because he became weak. Keith had wanted to run away, leave all this behind, start over.

LAWMAN

Ned knew he couldn't start over until this was over. Jim Long had to die.

Ned watched the cluster of people start moving off toward town. He stood and went to his horse. He removed his canteen from the saddle horn. He took a drink. He sloshed the liquid around in the canteen, it was nearly empty.

He considered his options again. He put the stopper back in the canteen. He took the reins and stepped into the saddle.

He turned his horse and headed down the hill, toward town.

The streets were nearly empty as he entered town. Ned rode his horse slowly down the street.

He glanced over at the marshal's office. To go in there was a foolish move. He couldn't be foolish if he wanted to kill Marshal Long.

He reined up in front of the saloon. He dismounted, tied his horse to the rail, and went inside.

The saloon was empty as Ned walked in. The bartender recognized him as soon as he saw him. Ned pulled his gun, pointed it at Silas. "I'll need a bottle and a glass," he said, stepping to the bar.

Silas got a bottle and poured the drink. Ned struck Silas in the head hard enough to knock him off balance.

RONNIE ASHMORE

Ned grabbed him by the shirtfront and pulled him over the bar. Silas crashed to the floor in a heap. Ned hit him in the face with the butt of his pistol.

"Go get the marshal. Tell him I'm here." Silas got to his feet and went out the door on the run. Silas grabbed the whiskey bottle and the glass from the bar.

He walked to a table and sat down, waiting.

75

Long was startled as Silas came into the office in full force. He was bleeding from the face, it was all down the front of his shirt.

"What happened to you?"

Long stood, looking for a towel to stop some of the bleeding.

Silas pointed, ignoring the blood.

"He's at the saloon, Jim. Waiting for you. One of the twins..."

"Ned? He did this?"

Long slid the pistol from his holster, checking the loads, then reholstered. He went to the wall and pulled a short-barreled shotgun down from the rack. He loaded it as he looked out the open door toward the saloon.

"Anyone with him, Silas?"

"No. Just him. You want some help?"

"No. Find Morgan, he may be out at the ranch. Tell everyone else to stay out of it. Enough townsfolk have died to this bunch."

Silas left the office heading toward the livery and a horse. Long thought about what he should do next.

RONNIE ASHMORE

As soon as he went into the saloon, he would be a target. Ned would shoot at first sight and probably would get the best of the fight no matter how fast Long would shoot.

There was no good solution to this situation. All that talk about justice and laws that he had given Levi Goren at the start of this seemed foolish now.

At the saloon was a man who was as much a predator as anything in nature. He didn't care about the polite society or laws or any of that. He was a killer.

Long stepped outside. He scanned the streets and was glad no one seemed to be out and about.

The saloon had only one window. Long stepped to his right to cross the street and avoid being seen from that window.

As he crossed the street, he felt his heart hammering in his ears. His hands were sweaty as he held the shotgun pointed in front of him. He dared not wipe his hands off. He took a deep breath to control his breathing and try to calm his nerves.

He stepped onto the boardwalk and placed his back to the wall of the saloon. Taking careful steps, he eased his way to the swinging doors of the saloon.

He strained to hear any sounds from inside. A horse neighed causing Long to turn toward the livery. It was Silas on a horse heading out of town. Long took a deep breath again, silently cursing himself.

LAWMAN

At the door of the saloon, Long readjusted his grip on the shotgun. He dove through the door, hitting the ground and rolling coming to a knee, the shotgun ready, Long ready to shoot any target.

Long looked around the saloon. No one was there.

76

Ned heard the doors of the saloon crash open. He stood in the alley at the back of the saloon listening. Smiling to himself, he made his way around piles of trash and debris that was piled up along the back of the building.

He turned into an alley that would lead to the main road. He stopped. He had no desire to go walking down the main street of town yet. He backtracked to the rear of another business. He looked for another way to get around.

Farther behind the businesses there was a little gully that probably only held water when it rained. It was dry now. Ned considered taking it, but just as fast dismissed the idea. He would not slink in the weeds like a snake.

He laughed quietly to himself. Shaking his head, he went back to the mouth of the alley and faced the main street.

He pulled his pistol, thinking for a moment. Where could he go? Keeping concealed to avoid being seen by the few people walking on the streets, he looked for a way.

He nodded his head as if he had just reached a major decision. He would go where he wanted and anyone who confronted him on the street would die. Simple as that.

The marshal would be coming along in a moment, he needed to decide now.

He started to step out into the street. Movement at the hotel stopped him. That woman stood there on the porch.

LAWMAN

She was the reason his friends were all dead. She would have to die as well.

Ned stepped from the alley into the street. He stepped up on the boardwalk and walked slowly along, his pistol at his side.

He was smiling in anticipation of putting a bullet in that woman's head, blowing her brains out and wrecking whatever beauty she had for all time.

Ned stopped walking as she turned her head as she placed a hat on her head. She looked off, then back quickly.

Ned lifted the gun and fired a fast shot at the woman. The bullet hit the support post of the hotel porch. He cocked the hammer for a second shot. The woman was gone.

Ned stepped off the boardwalk into the street. He cursed himself for missing that shot. She was right there, a sitting duck, and he had missed.

The few people that were out in the street were taking shelter where they could. The men protecting the women and children.

Ned looked around for a threat. The men would not cower down long. They would fight, just like last time.

He had a decision to make. The woman or marshal, he couldn't kill both. He ran across the street opposite the alley he had been in. He ran into the alley on this side of the road.

He was confused and distracted. He also knew he had to move more decisively. His presence was known now, the men in town would know he was back, and the marshal was coming.

He slapped his hand on his leg in frustration. He should have planned this better.

77

Long looked around the bar. He held the shotgun ready as he walked to the back door of the building.

He stepped out into the alley quietly, taking care to make as little noise as he could. The alley was empty.

He saw a jumble of boot tracks. Some facing this way, some that way, as if the man who had made them was walking in circles.

He started to follow them when he heard the pistol shot and the screams.

Running down the alley, he came to the main street. He saw some men and women ducking inside stores to safety. Some of the men came back into the street. Looking for the danger.

Long stepped out into the street, shotgun in hand. He motioned the men back inside.

One of the men jerked his head toward the alley across the street. Long looked that way but saw nothing.

He walked across the street to the alley, keeping watch as he did. To his left was his office. Movement from that direction caught his eye.

Ned had circled the buildings from behind, he stepped into the street next to the marshal's office.

As Long turned to fire, he felt the wind by his ear flutter as a bullet buzzed past.

RONNIE ASHMORE

Dropping to a knee Long fired one barrel of the shotgun. He knew he had missed as soon as he shot. Ned had taken cover behind the wall of the building.

Long moved back into the alley for cover as he reloaded the shotgun. He looked around for Jacob Keith. Silas only mentioned Ned being in the saloon, but surely Keith wouldn't send Ned into town alone, would he?

Long needed to know. He eased back into the street, watching for movement.

"Where's your boss, Ned?"

"Dead, marshal, just like you and that woman will be in a few minutes."

Ned's voice sounded strange, though Long had not heard him talk much. He sounded excited, or was he scared?

"You killed Jacob Keith?"

"I did and I burned his house down too. Now enough talkin'. I got killin' to do."

Long was moving as Ned was talking. He went behind the buildings and ran until he heard Ned stop talking. He slowed to a walk, stepping lightly, making no noise. Ned was around the corner from where he now stood. He needed surprise on his side, or the gunman might not miss a second shot.

"You gonna die, lawman."

Long stepped around the corner. The distance was less than ten feet. Ned was facing the street, pistol in hand.

LAWMAN

"You're under arrest."

Long's voice was loud in the silence of the moment. Ned spun around trying to get his gun into action.

Long fired both barrels of the shotgun into Ned. Ned's chest and throat disintegrated into a bloody mess of tissue and fluid. Ned was thrown backwards due to the blast. He fell on the ground, not moving.

Long walked up to look down on the dead outlaw. Ned's eyes stared unseeing up at Long.

"You should have stayed out of my town," Long said, bending to pick up the dead man's gun.

78

They sat around the table at the Rafter R, laughing, talking, enjoying each other's company and the time they had to spend.

Martha, as was her custom, had prepared the meal for the dinner, though to Long and Morgan's surprise, she had let Frannie help some.

As Levi passed the apple pie to Morgan, Martha sipped her tea, and said,

"So, Clara, when will school begin?"

Clara placed her fork on her plate, looked around the table.

"With everything seeming to settle down, I'm hoping to begin Monday morning."

"So soon?" Morgan said. "How many kids do you think will show up?"

Clara looked down at her plate, then back up at Morgan.

"I don't know. I have had a lot of parents tell me they would be sending their children though."

"I know from talk about town, there are a lot of people who respect you for standing strong from what you went through," Long said.

"I didn't feel so strong when he shot at me on the hotel porch. I ran back inside scared to death."

LAWMAN

"I don't blame you for that at all," Frannie said, refilling everyone's coffee cup.

"You showed sand, Clara. True sand."

Clara looked at Levi, then said,

"Sand?"

Levi looked around the table, smiling an embarrassed smile. He was greeted by grins from everyone.

"Means you'll do to ride the river with ma'am," Morgan said.

Clara laughed.

"I am not going to be riding any rivers for a while."

Everyone laughed.

"Speaking of the future. What are your plans? I assume you'll be married?"

Levi and Clara looked at Martha, then back at each other.

"I ain't got a thing to offer her, but I am going to marry her. I'll figure out something to do in town maybe."

"Well, speaking of that, I believe Morgan had a good idea," Martha said, pointing at Morgan, who looked surprised.

All eyes were on him, he swallowed a bite of pie and said,

RONNIE ASHMORE

"Well, we need help here on the ranch. It seems you know cows pretty well and I could use the extra help what with me deputying as well as being here."

Levi looked at Clara. He was as shocked as she seemed to be. Both were outsiders to this place, yet both had found family and friends that would last a lifetime.

"If there is enough work for me here, then I accept."

Martha nodded, then said,

"Well, there is nothing left to discuss but the wedding."

"Martha, let them get settled down a bit first," Frannie said.

"Oh, I wasn't meaning theirs," she said, looking from Frannie to Long.

Long caught the look, he stared at his mother, then at Frannie. He took a bite of pie.

ABOUT THE AUTHOR

Ronnie Ashmore is the author of several books in the western and police mystery genres. His primary focus is the western genre where his books are packed with realism and grit.

When not writing he enjoys playing golf, traveling, and spending time with his family.

MORE FROM RONNIE ASHMORE

Colby PD Series
Family Secrets
Colby Nights

John Riley Bounty Hunter Series
The Losing Trail
The Killing Trail
The Vengeance Trail
The Deceiving Trail
A Bullet for Malo
The Claren Range Dispute

Sam Bolton Ex Ranger
Duty Bound
Fighting Men
Crooked Trail

Other Books
Last Stand for a Bad Man
Texas: 1857

Non-Fiction
Lessons on Leadership:
Leading Behind the Badge

Jim Long
Homecoming

ABOUT THE AUTHOR

Ronnie Ashmore is the author of several books in the western and police mystery genres. His primary focus is the western genre where his books are packed with realism and grit. A former police officer and two time Chief of Police, he writes with an authority of the places and the people of his stories. When not writing he enjoys playing golf, traveling, and spending time with his family.

ABOUT THE PUBLISHER

Creative Texts is a boutique independent publishing house devoted to high quality content that readers enjoy. We publish best-selling authors such as Ronnie Ashmore, Jerry D. Young, N.C. Reed, Sean Liscom, Jared McVay, Laurence Dahners, and many more. Our audiobook performers are among the best in the business including Hollywood legends like Barry Corbin and top talent like Christopher Lane, Alyssa Bresnaham, Erin Moon and Graham Hallstead.

Whether its post-apocalyptic or dystopian fiction, biography, history, true crime science fiction, thrillers, or even classic westerns, our goal is to produce highly rated customer preferred content. If there is anything we can do to enhance your reader experience, please contact us directly at info@creativetexts.com. As always, we do appreciate your reviews on your book seller's website.

Finally, if you would like to find more great books like this one, please search for us by name in your favorite search engine or on your bookseller's website to see books by all Creative Texts authors.

Thank you for reading!

Made in the USA
Columbia, SC
05 November 2023

25067058R00134